WHAT
SHAPES
THESE
CLOUDS

alex gregor

Orbis Tertius Press

Alberta, Canada

Published by Orbis Tertius Press

Original artwork by Sean Riley
Front cover image: *Straight Forward*, 2024 / oil on paper, 15.5" x 9.5"
Back cover image: *All There Is*, 2024 / oil on paper, 15.5" x 9.5"
seanrileystudio.com

ISBN: 978-1-0688637-1-4

alla mia famiglia romana

(soprattutto i pignetini)

CONTENTS

somewhere between the fog and the dew is the cloud. climb the mountain path until you're short of breath; there, you'll see it, perched upon the peak. or, ride the ocean's waves to the doldrums, where the sun will ferry you to its doors.

What Shapes These Words

On the day the volcano erupted, I was born.

Your body, shattered into a million pieces, was scattered across this land.

Waters rose up out of the ground and filled the space you left behind.

Waters rose up out of the sea and fell from the clouds that rolled across the sky.

~~~

I hear there is something inside of you.

Some say there is a sunken village.

Some say there is a fountain of gold.

Others say there is an undetonated bomb.

~~~

Some days, I can hear you speaking with the fish, your voice filling their mouths.

Other days, I can hear you whispering to the trees, your words taking shape on their leaves.

Other days still, I can hear you singing with the birds, your song echoing through the hills.

~~~

I've taken on new shapes in your absence.

Winds blow across me; the moon tugs.

Stones are polished into sand.

~~~

I came to the lake neither for the sunken village, nor the fountain, nor the bomb, but for the birds.

I followed them out of the city, where they flew over the hills and dove into the water below.

~~~

It's been what seems like 1,000 years, but they still have not emerged.

~~~

What has emerged are the leaves.

They rise up from the lake bottom and float on the surface before sinking back down to the eels.

~~~

What's written on these leaves are words of a language I have never seen before.

~~~

I am convinced the clouds are behind this.

The shapes they take on in the sky above me.

The rain they carry from the sea.

~~~

There is something about these words, when I feed them into my typewriter, that causes my boat to move more swiftly across the water.

~~~

There is something about these words, when I feed them back into the water, that causes the wind to pick up and blow harder across the surface of the lake.

~~~

I can feel something taking shape inside of me.

It is dense and amorphous.

It swells in the night—so much that I cannot sleep.

I lie awake and listen to it breathing.

During the day, it hums.

Sometimes I hum with it.

I can feel its current passing through mine.

~~~

I've noticed recently, when feeding these words into my typewriter, that my mouth has been taking on their shapes.

And so, I have been feeding these words into the sky.

~~~

Perhaps the clouds will carry these words to the sea, where they will wash up onto the beach with the tides.

Perhaps the clouds will carry these words to the mountains, where they will sink down into the aquifer.

Perhaps the clouds will carry these words to the cities, where they will form puddles in the streets.

Perhaps someone will stop and stare into these puddles.

I wonder what shapes these words will take on.

somewhere between the ice and the steam is the water. stand beneath the clouds as they hang heavy above your head; sit along the canal as the wind blows up the coast; lay in your hammock as the moon and sun tug upon the ocean—there, you'll feel it: falling in sheets, rising up your legs, carrying you out to sea.

ALONG THE
LUNGOMARE

What Shapes These Clouds

If you follow the *lungomare*—the road that hugs the sea—from Ostia to Circeo, you will see abandoned factories, rundown beach resorts, and waterfront restaurants. In Sabaudia, there is a restaurant made entirely of fallen trees, and the people inside built it with their bare hands years ago, when the pontine was still a swamp, before the fascists filled it in.

These people—a family of four—left Rome by train. When they reached the mouth of the Tevere, where the river spills out into the sea, they took a bus south until they came to an inlet. This was as far as the bus would go. But along the banks were little wooden rowboats tied up to pylons, so they borrowed one to paddle across. After tying up on the other side, the family crossed the dunes and the reeds until they came to a beach.

In the late afternoon, they arrived at a strip of sand where towering umbrella pines had been uprooted by a storm. The surf had climbed up the beach, where a patch of trees had stood gallantly in the marsh, and as the soil eroded from under their roots, they came crashing down. Over time, from the changing tides and coastal winds, these trees became partially covered by sand, so that their trunks and branches had taken on the appearance of massive bones sticking out of the ground and reaching up into the skies.

The family, they took one look at these trees and knew just what to do with them. From their bags, they pulled out axes and hacksaws and began to chop and saw through the wood until each tree had been cut into logs. With these logs, these people built their home.

It didn't take long for the money to run out. After all, the family had very little to begin with. But once it had, they collected more wood that had washed ashore and used it to build tables, chairs, and a sign that read: RISTORANTE. They knew the view would say the rest.

~~~

Over time, the restaurant made quite a name for itself, but only among the few who had driven down the coastline and stumbled upon the wooden sign hanging in the window. Those with an appetite, driving on the lungomare on their way to Sperlonga, Baia, or Napoli, would pull off on the side of the road, where the sand had blown in from the dunes onto the asphalt, climb out of their cars, and walk through the restaurant's doors.

Lone travellers would usually take a seat at the bar on one of the wooden stools. Couples would nearly always nestle into a nook by a window, overlooking the sea. Families—especially with kids—would take whatever was given to them, usually settling for a table in the corner, out of everyone's way.

The children would always be the first to notice them looking down from the rafters: the bill of a marlin spearing a mackerel, the claw of a crab snipping a fishing line, the eyes of a flounder seeming to gaze into their own.

"What are *those*?" the children would ask, pointing to the ceiling.

"What are *what*?" their parents would respond, looking over their shoulders.

"*Animals*, dear," the adults would explain. "Those are *animals*."

~~~

The father of the family who built the restaurant from fallen trees was nearly always the first to rise. He would wake up before the sun, get dressed, and make himself a coffee. Once the water had filtered through the grounds and spilled into the pot, he would pour himself a mug and head onto the dock to watch the sunrise.

But before all of this, when he had first woken up, he would lay in bed, under the sheets, with his eyes closed, and think. In these waking moments, the bed was a boat, without any oars or a sail, just an anchor that had been dropped down to the sandy bottom below.

He could feel the boat being tossed by the waves, the bow rising with the crests, the stern sliding down into the troughs. And he could hear the water sloshing against the gunwale, the rope going slack, and then tightening again as each wave tried to carry the boat away.

As the boat rocked with the waves, the father saw his thoughts in the sky above—clouds passing slowly in and out of his periphery. Sometimes these clouds took on the shapes of yesterday—fishing trips to Ponza, candlelit dinners, lakeside weddings. Sometimes these clouds took on the shape of the day ahead—checking the crab traps, watering the garden, cooking dinner. And sometimes, if the father was lucky, these clouds took on shapes of their own.

When they did, the father would open his eyes, reach for his notebook on his bedside table, pick up his pencil, and sketch out the shapes of these clouds.

~~~

Late at night, after the restaurant was closed and the family had eaten their dinner, the mother liked to walk out onto the beach and collect driftwood. She would push a little wheelbarrow, with a broad wooden wheel, across the firmly packed sand left behind by the receding tide, and when she saw a piece of wood, waterlogged and adorned in kelp and shellfish, she would kneel down and, in the dim light of her kerosene lamp, look into the driftwood and see what she saw.

What she saw depended on how the light of her lantern fell upon the bark, or how the seaweed was draped across the branches, or how the barnacles had adhered themselves to the contours of the limb. But if she saw something in the rings of the stump, or the roots of a tree, or a forgotten plank from some capsized vessel, she would scoop that wood up into her arms and lay it down carefully into the wheelbarrow.

In the comfort of her rocking chair that sat by the windows of the dining room, she would pull out a pocketknife from the front of her apron and begin to whittle. She would shave away the bark from this wood, carve notches into the crevices, and chip away at the limbs, until a branch with a fork became a swordfish, or a stray shingle became the shell of a clam, or a cluster of roots became an octopus. And when she was done, she would arrange them on a dining table, sweep up the wood shavings at her feet, return to her chair, and rock herself to sleep.

~~~

The son, when he went out fishing at night, liked to bring with him a bottle of amaro and his violin, which had been given to him by his great-grandfather, who had carved the instrument himself out of wood that he had chopped down near his home in the thick mountain forests of the Appenino Abruzzese. The great-grandfather had taught the boy how to restring his instrument with the dried-out intestines of sheep, how to re-hair his bow from the mane of a horse, and how to collect rosin from the trunk of a pine.

With his violin stored in a hard leather case, the son would paddle out into the sea. After rowing past the breakers, he would pick up a fishing pole with a trolling rig, stick the barb of the hook through the eye of a fish-head, then slowly let out the line behind the boat.

If he was lucky enough to pull his rig through a school of fish and the tip of his rod jerked down to the water's surface, he would drop his oars, pick up his pole, and reel it in. In the boat, he had a gaf and a net, so he could easily pull them over the gunwale and down into the bucket, where he'd keep them cool until returning to shore, where he would clean and fillet them before packing them on ice in the restaurant's kitchen.

Whether the fish went after the trolling rig or not didn't really matter, because he knew once he got out far enough, all he would have to do was drop his bait down, and it would just be a matter of time before his bucket was full.

But some nights, when the moon was full and the sea was calm, he wouldn't bait up his poles with anything at all. He would simply row out to where he knew they would be waiting. Once he got there, he would put down the oars quietly in the hull of the boat, uncork the bottle of amaro, pull out his violin, rosin up his bow, and begin to play.

And the fish, they would rise up to the surface, their eyes sticking out of the water, their mouths wide open, and their tails slowly moving back and forth. As the son played, he would, at times, look over the side into the water, where there weren't only fish, but plankton and calamari, shrimp and octopus, oysters and clams, bobbing up and down with the seawater, for as far as the son could see.

~~~

The daughter was a painter, and when she wasn't painting, she was out on the beach, foraging. Turtle eggs and cuttlefish ink, when mixed with crushed shell or stone, could be made into paint. The feathers of gulls and pelicans, when cleaned, could be made into brushes and pens. Nearly anything at all, the daughter was always discovering, could be used as a canvas.

From piles of driftwood that had collected in tidal pools along the beach, the daughter sifted. Some days, she pulled out the battered hull of a small boat very similar to her own brother's. Other days, she found vacant conch shells and withered starfish, trapped in netting. But one winter afternoon, when the sun was hanging low in the sky, and the wind was blowing hard, and the sea was churning like a stockpot in the restaurant's kitchen, coming to a roiling boil, the daughter unearthed something that she had never seen before.

Buried beneath a pile of rubbish and scraps at the base of Circeo, far down the beach from the family's restaurant, was a massive circular woodcut, waterlogged and beaten. The work of art was as large—if not larger—than the longest banquet table in their dining room, and the artwork itself was stunning: the figure of a man wearing a long robe and bristling beard, crouching on all fours to stick his head through the firmament of the Old World, the stars and planets rotating around the flat Earth, the well-oiled gears of the cosmos moving like clockwork among nebulous clouds.

The daughter, entranced by the image, grabbed the artwork along its edges and pulled, but it would not budge. From her satchel, she took out some rope, wrapped it around the wood, and heaved—but still, the piece would not move. She looked out at the horizon and knew just what to do. Digging deep into her bag, she pulled out an easel, her sketchbook, her pens and brushes, as well as some charcoal, ink, and paint. Standing over the woodcut, she used the charcoal to sketch the scene that lay before her.

She felt the sun's warmth on her back as she traced the firmament with a piece of charcoal, extending it to a globe. And the wind died down a bit when she drew a woman in the man's place, looking at the earth from the cosmos, rather than the other way around. And she heard the waves subside as she began drawing the oceans and the continents that divide them. She traced out the rivers, and filled in the lakes, and drew clouds of sand blowing across bodies of water to other continents, where the particles settled on the floor of forests and plains. Above these continents, she drew flying rivers that flowed from one ocean to another, where they eventually formed into ice and fell in sheets into the ocean, where a feast awaited.

Once she was done sketching, the daughter took out her paints and brushes and started painting over her drawing. Then, after cleaning her brushes in a jar of seawater and packing up, she headed back to the restaurant to get her family's help to move what she had found.

But by the time she returned with her father, mother, and brother, the woodcut had disappeared.

~~~

The family discovered the cave at the height of summer. They were walking along the beach—the father and mother foraging shellfish from the rocks, the son throwing his casting net into the shallows—when the daughter noticed the narrow opening at the base of the cliff. Once they had all crawled into the hole and stood up in the cavernous hall, the family could not believe what they saw: a sprawling mosaic of shell and bone, a subaquatic maritime mural of the creatures that swam beneath, and at the centre of it all hung the woodcut from the year before, exactly as the daughter had painted it.

The daughter opened her satchel and took out her sketchbook, comparing her work with what hung on the cave wall. The mother, setting down the bucket of shellfish on the cave floor, noticed that her wooden figurines were suspended from the cave ceiling, their eyes seeming to stare into her own. The son, taking a swig from his bottle of amaro, saw the fish floating on the surface in the mural, their mouths open, and he could hear them singing. The father, whose eyes were just now adjusting to the dim light of the cave, realized that the ceiling, walls, and floor were all covered in clouds—sky-fulls of them. There were towering cumulonimbus clouds, mushrooming above churning seas. There were the feathery fingers of cirrus clouds, reaching out across bright blue skies. There were low-hanging shelf clouds, rolling across coastal marshlands and estuaries. And as the father stood there, staring into these clouds, it began to rain.

In the light drizzle that fell from the ceiling of the cave, the son took out his violin and began to play, pulling the horsehair bow across sheep-gut strings, making them sing. The daughter, pulling out a tambourine from her satchel, joined her brother in a pizzica, tapping and shaking the instrument quickly between her hands. And as the parents danced in circles and turns on the floor of the cave, the mother's wooden figurines—swordfish, flounder, marlin, and mackerel; calamari, shrimp, crabs, and octopus; oysters, mussels, snails, and clams—began crawling down the walls of the cave into the pools of water that were forming on the cave floor, where the rising tide would carry them all back out to sea.

somewhere between the sea and the sand is the shell. stroll along the shore when the tide is going out; there, you'll see it, exposed by receding waves. or, listen to the wind blowing through its apertures when the tide is coming in—echoing through its spires and whorls: a resounding song.

These Seas That Swell

When you follow the *lungomare*—the road that hugs the sea—from Circeo to Gaeta, you will pass ancient ruins, hilltop temples, and waterfront restaurants. In Sperlonga, there is a restaurant made entirely of mud and grass, and the people inside built it with their bare hands years ago, when estuaries emptied out into the sea, before eroding topsoil dried them up.

These people—a family of four—left Sabaudia by boat. When they reached the Cave of Gaia, where the waves crashed onto the rocks of Mount Circeo, they filled up their nets and buckets with shellfish and anchovies, packed down their vessel with tools and supplies, and readied their boat to sail down the coast.

In the early afternoon, the family arrived at an estuary where water broth, both brackish and sweet, mixed between high banks of pluff mud and salt grass. The family, they took one look at this mud and this grass and knew what to do with it. From their boat, they pulled out shovels and buckets and began to dig. They drove their shovels deep down into the mud, heaving out hefty heaps until each of their buckets was full. Then, the family took out their shears and baskets and cut down the grass until each basket was full, too. With this mud and this grass, the family built their home.

It didn't take long for the supplies to run out. After all, there were few supplies to begin with. But after they had, the family collected more mud and grass from the estuary and used it to build tables, chairs, and a sign that read: RISTORANTE. They knew their food would do the rest.

~~~

Despite its location, the restaurant never quite made a name for itself. The locals and tourists alike preferred fine dining—large plates of seafood pasta presented elegantly on silver platters atop white tablecloths—but the family was committed to preparing simple, down-home dishes from all over the world: fried grouper and shrimp, blackened flounder and sea bass, low country boils and jambalayas, paellas and curries, phōs and gumbos, served up with ice-cold beer or chilled wine made in-house from local ingredients by the family.

Regardless, those with an appetite driving along the lungomare on their way to Pozzuoli, Ischia, or Amalfi would see the open-air beachfront establishment and stop for its charm. Regulars would usually take a seat at the bar on one of the stools. Teenagers would nearly always nestle into a nook on the patio, overlooking the estuary. Tourists—especially with children—would take whatever was given to them, usually settling for a table in the corner, out of everyone's way.

The adults would be the first to see them: a cluster of mangrove roots hanging from the ceiling, a bouquet of saltwort sprouting from the centre of the table, a patch of seagrass rooted in the mud floors.

"What are *those*?" the adults would ask, pouring themselves another glass of wine.

"What are *what*?" the children would respond, their mouths full of fried fish.

"*Those*," the parents would say, raising their glasses to their mouths.

"*Those*," the children would explain, sipping their sodas, "are *plants*."

"*Plants*," the adults would echo, nodding their heads up and down slowly, repeating the words that came from their children's mouths. "Those are *plants*."

~~~

When the tide was rising in the early afternoon, the mother of the family that had built the restaurant from mud and grass liked to sit on the banks of the estuary and watch it fill with seawater. After finishing her lunch, she would enjoy a hand-rolled cigarette and amaro in her rocking chair on the restaurant's patio, and then grab her coat and stroll down the beach.

On her way to the estuary, the mother would pass the tidal pools, filled with starfish, shellfish, and minnows, which the rising tides would carry back out to sea. She would also pass the magnificent sand dunes, crawling with saltwort and sand reed, where crabs were scurrying in and out of their burrows in the sun.

While the tides and the dunes interested the mother, what had drawn her away from the restaurant down the beach wasn't the estuary itself, but the mud that lined its banks. This mud—a pungent, viscous miasma—was crawling with life. The salt grass grew up out of it along the banks, and the oysters rooted to it in the shallows; the fiddler crabs burrowed into it on the shore; and the flounder buried themselves in it on the estuary bottom. And it was with this mud that the mother made her sculptures.

With a small trowel that she carried in her apron, she would scoop out heaps of this mud onto the banks as the seawater spilled into the estuary, carrying with it larger fish, crustaceans, and debris, and she would mould this mud into shapes.

What shapes the mother moulded the heaps into depended on what she saw in the estuary that day. Some days, her sculptures took on the shapes of driftwood, adorned with barnacles and kelp. Other days, her sculptures took on the shapes of flounder, the strange flat fish with both eyes on the same side of its head.

Regardless of what the mother saw in the estuary on any given day, she would always sculpt a starling from the mud, reminding herself of Rome.

~~~

Late in the evening, when the tide was out, the daughter liked to forage on the beach in the tide pools. After she had finished dinner and poured herself a final glass of wine, she would grab her satchel from her desk and head out into the night.

The daughter always thought that the beach, at night, when the tide was fully out, looked like the surface of the moon—sand that had been smoothed by receding waves, tide pools carved out by the shifting currents, the entire scene a vast monochromatic landscape illuminated by celestial bodies, passing boats, and the occasional bioluminescent plankton bloom in the swash zone —and it was upon this strange, mysterious landscape that the daughter foraged for shells.

On her nightly passeggiata, the daughter would find shells from conchs, clams, and snails; shells from scallops, mussels, and oysters; shells from crabs, lobsters, and, every now and then, the shell of a nautilus. And when she found these shells, she would stoop down and scoop them up in her hands— or sometimes in her arms, if they were too large to pick up with her hands alone—and place them into her satchel.

The daughter would scavenge the beach for shells until she reached the estuary, where she would sit down on a flat rock and take these shells out— one by one—and skip them across the surface of the water. The daughter would do this, skipping the shells and counting the number of times they graced the surface, until her satchel was empty.

~~~

At high tide in the late afternoon, the son liked to go fishing. Long before preparing dinner, when the sun was just beginning to drop in the sky, he would grab his casting net and buckets, and walk down to the estuary to see what the tides had brought in that day.

The son would walk up and down the banks, surveying the surface for signs of bait-fish swimming in schools. When he saw them, he would ready the casting net in both of his hands, feeling the weights between his fingers, and then he would toss it. The son would throw that casting net out across that water in such a way that it would open up, as wide as the mouth of the estuary itself, and swallow up whatever was inside. Standing on the bank with the rope in hand, the son would then slowly tug until he could empty it out onto the sand around his feet.

When he opened that net, out would fall minnows, mackerel, flounder, bass, crabs, and shrimp—dancing and flopping around on the sand like they had fallen right into the son's frying pan in the restaurant's kitchen. This is when he would scoop up his catch, one by one, and throw them into his bucket, which he had filled with water from the sea.

Once his bucket was full, he would walk further down the banks of the estuary until he came to the outdoor kitchen that he had built with his sister years before. In this kitchen, the son would clean the fish—scraping the scales from their bodies, emptying the guts from their bellies, and separating the meat from the bone as he portioned them out into fillets. Later, he would carry his catch back to the restaurant. He would keep them on ice until that night's dinner, when he would steam the shellfish and batter down and fry up the fillets; he would toss them in sauce, season them heavily, and throw them on platters for himself, his family, and whomever else had stopped by the restaurant that day.

But before he went back to the restaurant, the son would take those guts and scales and plant them shallow in the pluff mud, where the family had harvested the salt grass. He would take his hand and hollow out a little hole in the mud, drop in some of the innards from the fish and a single fish scale, and then cover the hole up again. He did this until each of the scales that had been scraped from the bodies of the fish had been planted. When he was done, he would rinse off his hands in the brackish water, grab his bucket, and head home.

~~~

Early in the morning, when the tide was going out, the father of the family liked to go for a swim. After drinking a cup of tea in the restaurant's kitchen, he would descend the steps from the dining room to the beach and walk along the shoreline until he came to an estuary. Here, he would wade out into the sea until he could no longer walk. It was then that he would swim.

Beginning with a dive into a wave, he would swim underwater for as long as he could hold his breath. Then, he would surface past the breakers and begin to move parallel to the shoreline, leisurely at first, starting with a breaststroke, then switch to a backstroke, and end in a butterfly.

After he had worn himself out, he would flip over onto his back, take a deep breath in, and hold it. With this breath in his lungs, the father would float. He would lay on his back on the rolling waves—his head and torso on the surface, his legs and feet dangling in the water beneath him—and he would look into the sky above.

Sometimes, the sky above would be bright blue as far as the father could see, without a single cloud. Other times, the sky above would be filled with a dense layer of shelf clouds, bringing in the rain from far off the coast. But every now and then, when the weather was just right, the sky above would be both blue and filled with clouds. On these days, the father would lay on his back with his lungs filled with air, his body suspended in the seawater, and watch the shapes that these clouds took on.

Some days, these clouds took on the shapes of animals: an opossum, hanging upside down by its tail in a tree; a raccoon, fishing for crawdads in a shallow creek. Other days, these clouds would take on the shapes of plants: sprawling live oaks draped in Spanish moss; towering umbrella pines on rolling hills. But no matter the day, after the father had been floating on his back in the sea for a long time—breathing in through his nose, holding it, and slowly letting the air out of his mouth, again and again—these clouds took on shapes of their own. When they did, the father would open up his mouth and begin to sing.

~~~

The father discovered the statue at low tide at the beginning of autumn, after a week of tempestuous storms. He was walking up the beach towards the estuary for his morning swim when he saw a trident jutting out of the sand. When he returned with his family later, they took one look at the statue and knew just what to do.

With their shovels, the family dug the statue out and dragged it over to the estuary, where they mounted it upright on the highest bank. There they covered its surfaces with mud and grass, until what had once been a statue became an amorphous lump of clay. As the sun climbed high above them, the family worked the mud into their hands until they had sculpted a live oak tree, draped in moss.

The family stood back from their creation and stared at it in the autumn sun —its roots climbing down the estuary's banks into the water below, its trunk standing sturdily in the mud and the muck that surrounded its base, its limbs reaching up to the sky above—then, the family went along their way: the father waded out into the sea for a swim; the mother sat down along the banks to sculpt; the son and daughter, together, walked up and down the estuary, searching for oysters.

When the son and daughter found them, they took out their knives from their pockets and shucked these oysters open. In each of these oysters was a pearl, which they planted at the base of the oak tree made of mud at the mouth of the estuary overlooking the sea.

Of course, the son and daughter ate the meat in the oysters, letting them slide down the back of their throats and into their bellies. After, the son passed his shells to the daughter, who slipped them into her pocket with hers.

That night, when the daughter went foraging under the light of the moon, she noticed the first leaves sprouting out of the limbs of the live oak. To this, she took the oyster shells from her pocket and skipped them across the water —but to her surprise, they did not sink. After they had skimmed the surface four times, they made their final splash and then floated. They must have floated for over an hour as the daughter sat there, watching, until eventually —when the tides changed and the saltwater spilled back into the estuary, slowly rising up the banks—these oyster shells suddenly sank down to the muddy bottom below.

somewhere between the wood and the leaves is the mushroom. wander the forest during a storm; turn over a log and trace the mycelium to the root. wait for thunder. when lightning strikes, follow the glowing path to the mouth of the river to where it spills into a lake. swim out to the floating fortress.

What Shapes These Birds

As you follow the *lungomare*—the road that hugs the sea—from Gaeta to Pozzuoli, you will see crater lakes, cliffside villages, and waterfront restaurants. In Baia, one of these restaurants is made entirely of sea glass and the people inside built it with their bare hands years ago, when the town was still a port, before it fell into the sea.

These people—a family of four—left Sperlonga by boat. They paddled down the coast until they reached the volcanic island of Ischia, where hot water springs bubble up from the sea floor into rocky tidal pools, and it was here that the family turned the bow toward the mainland and paddled into the bay.

In the back of this bay, there was a black sand beach covered in pebbles, shells, and driftwood. But strewn throughout these pebbles, these shells, and this driftwood were a million shards of smooth, opaque sea glass, glimmering in the sun.

The family took one look at this sea glass and knew just what to do with it. Walking up and down the beach, they collected it, shard by shard, placing it into piles. It was with these shards of sea glass that the family built their home.

It didn't take long for the rains to come. After all, the clouds had been mushrooming over the peak of Vesuvio for months before a single drop had fallen. But one day, the sky opened up, and down came the cats and dogs. When they did, the family collected more sea glass from the black sand beach and made a mosaic to hang in the window that read: RISTORANTE. They knew their service would say the rest.

~~~

The restaurant quickly became popular among locals and tourists alike, not just for the service but also for the location. From every single table in the dining room, there was a panoramic view of the coast and the sea—from Napoli and Vesuvio to the islands of Procida and Ischia—and because of this, the guests didn't care where they sat. If they were travelling down the lungomare and saw the restaurant made of sea glass perched up on the side of the cliff, they would walk through the doors and sit down at whichever table they were given.

Regardless of where the people had come from or where they were headed, the elders would always be the first to notice them: a bespectacled face with eyebrows furrowed; a bristling beard, unkempt and burly; a mouthful of mussels, hanging ajar.

"What are *those*?" the elders would ask, tilting their heads to the side with a glass of wine in hand.

"What are *what*?" their grown children would respond, throwing fried calamari into their mouths.

"*Those*," the grandchildren would explain, staring calmly out to sea, "are *people*."

"*People*," the elders would echo, trying to mimic what their grandchildren had said. "Those. are. *people*."

~~~

After it rained, the mother loved to climb the hills around the bay and draw. What the mother drew depended on what she saw, and what she saw depended on what kind of rain had fallen from the sky that day: heavy rains would wash out the soil underneath the rocks on the hills and expose stones and shells, and sometimes even shards of pottery and chunks of bone; lighter rains would draw the insects from their burrows—slugs and snails, gnats and mosquitoes—and with the insects would come those that ate them—geckos and hedgehogs scurrying along the ground, sparrows and swifts swooping down from the skies.

But when the weather was just right and the clouds were hanging in the sky and the wind was blowing along the coast, the mother would see what interested her the most: the starlings. These birds flew in murmurations—large, shapeshifting flocks that stretched from one horizon to the other—and when she saw them, she would take her sketchbook from her satchel and draw. With a small pencil in hand, the mother would draw the shapes that these starlings took.

Sometimes, these starlings took on the shapes of clouds. Other times, these starlings took on the shapes of trees. No matter the shape, the mother always imagined them as schools of fish—shoals of them—moving through the sky as if it were the sea.

At night, when the rest of the family was sleeping, the mother would sit at a table in the dining room of the restaurant with a glass of wine and read from her sketchbook. Carefully flipping through the pages, the mother would read the shapes that the starlings had taken that day. Then, with her pencil in between her fingers, the mother would translate these shapes until each murmuration became a word became a phrase became a poem. And with each of these poems, the mother would roll them into small scrolls, stick them into the empty bottle from which she was pouring her wine, and cork it.

In the morning, before the sun rose out of the volcano, when the water in the bay was calm and clear, she would drop this bottle into a tide pool so that the rising waters would carry it out to sea.

~~~

The son of the family who had built the restaurant from sea glass loved to sing right before it rained. No matter the time of day or night, when he saw the clouds rolling in from the sea, he would wait for them to fill up and hang heavy over the bay. Once they had, he would grab his tambourine, descend the steps that led from the restaurant to the beach, and stroll. Under these clouds, the son would walk up and down the beach—past tide pools full of starfish and minnows, past jetties where oysters and mussels were clinging to the rocks, past sand dunes where ghost crabs were scurrying into their burrows—until he heard a note. From somewhere in the depths of the tide pools, or the crevices of the jetties, or the slopes of the dunes, the son would hear a single, solitary note. With this note, the son would write a melody, so that what was once a note became a phrase and a tune became a song. While tapping his fingers on the skin of the tambourine and shaking the rim so that the cymbals jangled between his fingers, the son would hum this song would whistle this song would sing this song—until it began to rain.

~~~

Whether it was raining or not, the father loved to cook in the kitchen of the restaurant. Whenever he had an appetite, he would go to the ice box and the pantry and look inside them both until he could imagine a meal. The meal he imagined depended on what the family had caught in the sea, foraged on the beach, or hunted in the hills. If the son had landed a black grouper from the underwater caves of Ischia and cleaned the fish and laid out the fillets in the icebox, then the father would see the fish sizzling in a cast iron skillet swimming in butter, lemon, and spices. If the daughter had speared squid in the bay and sliced them into rings, then the father would see the beer-battered calamari crisping to a golden brown in the deep fryer. If the mother had foraged blue crabs from the tidal pools that filled with seawater on the beaches, then the father would see them boiling in a pot with potatoes, corn on the cob, and sausages for a low country boil.

But no matter what was in the pantry or the ice box, the father would always imagine something to eat. And once he had, he would pull out the ingredients, lay them out carefully on the island that sat in the middle of the kitchen overlooking the sea, and begin to cook. Moving from the island to the sink to the stovetop to the deep fryer, the father would clean, cut, and mix his ingredients, slowly preparing a meal.

When the meal was ready, the father would reach for the rope that was tied to the bell that hung above the restaurant's bar that looked over the dining room, and he would ring it. The father would ring the bell so that everyone in the dining room would hear it. And when they did, they would line up at the bar of the restaurant with their plates, ready for the feast.

~~~

When it was raining, the daughter loved to go diving. With a fishing spear in one hand and a net in the other, she would push off the shore in the family's boat and paddle out into the bay until she came to a place where she had never dived before. Once she arrived, she would drop the anchor and jump from the stern of the boat into the water to the sandy bottom below.

As she sank, the daughter would look up and see the rain fall in sheets upon the surface, always reminding her of the stockpot in the family's kitchen filled with her catch of the day, coming to a roiling boil.

But when her feet touched the bottom, the daughter would look straight ahead and walk. Through forests of kelp and sea urchins, shoals of fish and squid; beneath islands of floating plastic; atop heaping mounds of aluminium —the daughter would walk along the bay bottom, spearing, until her net was full.

~~~

One day, when the daughter dove down to the bay bottom during a storm, she noticed that instead of sand beneath her feet, there were cobblestones. And as she walked across them, she saw that far off in the distance, there was a city.

The daughter walked across those cobblestones—through the kelp and the urchins, the fish and the squid, the plastic and the aluminium, the islands and mounds of trash—until she came to the city's gates. Within the walls were foundations of villas, the remnants of gutters and wells, and in the city centre, a piazza filled with very large statues: sea creatures wrapping their tentacles around three-masted ships; cloaked astronomers gazing into the heavens with their telescopes; children suckling on the teats of she-wolves; hourglasses and sundials, obelisks and crosses; cubes and pyramids, arches and columns.

As the daughter stood there staring in awe at what lay before her, she noticed that the sea urchins were slowly crawling up these statues. As the daughter stood there staring, she noticed that shoals of squid were quickly swimming into the piazza.

When the statues were covered completely by the urchins, and the daughter was surrounded entirely by squid, a cloud of ink descended upon her, causing the entire bay to turn black.

~~~

When the rains stopped, the daughter paddled the boat out into the bay to show her family what she had found earlier that year. Beneath blue skies and white clouds, the family dove—one by one—off the bow of the boat into the clear water and down into the depths.

On the bay bottom, the daughter led the family through the kelp forests, crawling with sea urchins and squid. On the bay bottom, the daughter led the family under islands of plastic and over mounds of aluminium. On the bay bottom, the daughter led the family along the cobblestone path that led to the city.

Inside the city's walls, the family passed the foundations of the villas and the remnants of gutters and wells; however, when they arrived in the piazza in the city centre, there were neither sea creatures nor ships, astronomers nor telescopes, children nor she-wolves; there were neither hourglasses nor sundials, obelisks nor crosses; there were no cubes, pyramids, arches, or columns anywhere in sight.

In their place was the family's boat, made entirely of sea glass. And inside that boat was the family, made entirely of sea glass, too.

The family took one look at this and had no idea what to do with it. They just bent their knees and pushed off the bottom until they were floating on the water's surface. Bobbing up and down in the water of the bay, they looked up to the skies, only to see murmurations of starlings flying out of the mouth of the volcano overhead.

somewhere between the sap and the resin is the wood. chop down the tree and stare into the stump. there, you'll see it, written in the rings. or, burn the logs in the hearth and follow the plume to the sea, where a pile of driftwood is adorned with barnacles and kelp.

What Fills These Wells

Follow the *lungomare*—the road that hugs the sea—from Napoli to Rome, and you'll see two clusters of islands in the Tyrrhenian: the Phlegraean Islands in the Gulf of Naples and the Pontine Islands off the coast of Circeo. If you take a boat from the mainland to the latter, you will arrive in the Port of Ponza, where there is a restaurant made entirely of tin. The people inside built it with their bare hands years ago, when the waters from the Atlantic flowed freely through the Strait of Gibraltar, before the nationalists built their dam.

These people—a family of four—left Baia by boat. They sailed out of the gulf, past Procida and Ischia, past Gaeta and Circeo, past Santo Stefano and Ventotene, until they came to Ponza, where abandoned hotels and dilapidated docks lined the shore.

In the back of the port, where cave mouths opened up to sandy beaches, there were stacks of sheet metal covered in barnacles, netting, kelp, and rust. The family took one look at this metal and knew just what to do with it. From their bags, they pulled out hammers and nails, and one by one, they pieced together this tin until they had constructed a home.

It didn't take long for the rust from this tin to settle into the lungs of the family. After all, the sheet metal had laid in the sun and rain for years without being moved. But now that it served as the walls and the ceilings of the home, it was falling in flakes and specks onto their furniture and floors.

To this, the family collected pumice stones that had washed ashore and scrubbed them against the metal until it was clean. With this rust, the family made a bright red paint by mixing it with turtle eggs and seawater.

In large, broad strokes on the side of their home, the family painted the word: RISTORANTE. They knew that the food and drinks they served to the captains and crews they would lure into the port would say the rest.

~~~

The restaurant became the best-kept secret among those that travelled down the coastline trawling for seafood, dumping refuse, transporting tourists, or rescuing migrants swimming from the mainland to the shores of North Africa. All the food and drinks served in the restaurant were harvested from the soil that had collected on the island's surfaces, or caught from the waters that crashed upon the island's rocky cliffs, or captured in nets from the air that surrounded the island's peaks—and for this reason, these captains and these crews would nearly always steer their helms toward the harbour, tie up to a buoy, and paddle their dinghies to shore for a feast.

From their seats—whether stools at the bar, chairs at banquet tables, or benches in booths—the newcomers would look around the restaurant in awe at the spectacle that surrounded them: honeycombs hanging from tree branches, swarming with bees; massive fossilized stumps, crawling with buzzing cicadas; orchestras of grasshoppers, rosining up their bows.

With their mouths ajar and their eyes squinted, these newcomers would turn their heads toward their crew in confusion.

"*What* in the *hell* are *those*?" the newcomers would ask, taking gulps of honeysuckle mead.

"What in the hell are *what*?" a skipper would respond, sucking a shrimp head dry.

"*Those*," the captain would respond, cracking the claw of a crab, "are *insects*."

"*Insects*," the newcomers would repeat below their breath, slowly. "*Those— are—insects*."

~~~

In the spring, clusters of wild bees would leave their hives and hang from the trees and bushes that grew along the beaches, cliffs, and peaks of the island. This is when the daughter of the family who had built the restaurant out of tin would take her tin bee houses from the shed at the back of the restaurant that overlooked the harbour and walk the footpaths that crossed the island until she heard the bees buzzing.

When the daughter heard these bees, her ears would perk up in the wind, and she would follow the sound until she saw them—droves of them, crawling on dead tree trunks, clustering on blossoming bushes, hanging on olive branches with newly-sprouted leaves—and when she did, she would crouch down on the ground where they were clustering and look at the shapes that these bees took on.

Sometimes, these bees took on the shapes of the stars—constellations hanging in the firmament. Other times, these bees took on the shapes of the birds—murmurations of starlings flying above the Eternal City in winter. Other times still, these bees took on the shapes of the clouds—enormous balls of cotton mushrooming above the churning sea.

If the daughter, crouching in the dirt below these bees, saw shapes in the swarms that resonated with her, she would open up her tin bee house and carefully lure the insects inside.

~~~

When the bees were busy filling up their pockets with pollen in the summer, schools of catfish would swim up into the caves that opened up at the bases of the cliffs that overlooked the sea to escape the heat. This is when the father, who was a fisherman, would dive off the cliffs into the water and swim up into these caves with the catfish to noodle.

Swimming up and down the walls of the cave, diving down to the bottom and surveying the rocks, the father would search for a hole or crevice. When he found one, he would stick his arm into it and feel for what was inside. Sometimes, when the father stuck his arm into a hole, he would feel sand and pebbles deposited by the tides. Other times, when the father slipped his arm into a crevice, he would feel a crab pinching his fingers. Other times still, when the father inserted his arm into a niche, he would feel an eel brush by his elbow.

But when the father was lucky, and the moon was full, and the flowers on the island were heavy with pollen, he would stick his arm into a hole or crevice inside one of these caves, and he would feel it: the gaping mouth of a massive saltwater catfish, hiding in the rocks. And when he did, he would slip his hand into the gills of this fish and pull it out.

In the restaurant's kitchen, the father would lay this catfish out on the cutting board and clean it. He would run the tip of his knife along the belly of this fish so that the guts would fall out into a bucket. Then, he would run the tip of his knife along the fish-head and remove the skin from the flesh. Finally, he would fillet it all out into pieces, which he would batter down and fry up in the deep fryer for himself, his family, and whoever else was in the restaurant that day.

After eating, the father would take the bucket—filled with the scales, skin, innards, and head—out to the garden. It was there that he would spread these scraps amongst the bones and the ash, and with his hoe, turn them over into the soil.

~~~

During the autumn, when the bees were collecting nectar from the season's final blossoms, the son would take the honey harvested from the hives by the daughter and make mead. By mixing honey with well-water and ripened grapes in large glass jugs, the son would create the base for the drink. Since the honey was filled with sugar and the ripened grapes were covered in wild yeast, they would ferment together in the jugs and become a golden, sparkling wine.

Depending on what had been harvested in abundance that year, the son would flavour the mead with other ingredients as well. Some years, the son would take dried flowers from a lavender plant or a rose bush and make a tea to add to his mead. Other years, the son would take blackberries and rasp-berries, which had hung heavy on the vines in the sun on the cliffs, and make a juice to add to his mead. One summer, the son traded a bottle of the previous fall's batch for a burlap sack filled with ginger root, which he mashed into a pulp, giving his mead a zesty kick.

But regardless of what was harvested in abundance on the island or traded in the harbour with passing ships, once each jug was filled to the brim with the ingredients, the son would carry them down to the cellar that the family had built into the side of the cliff that sat behind the restaurant in the harbour. Here, he would place them on the tin shelves that lined that cellar's walls and take out the airlocks from a drawer, inserting them into the mouth of each jug until they were sealed tight.

The next day, the son would return to the cellar to find the airlocks on the jugs gurgling—that wild yeast from the grapes was feasting on the sugar found in the honey, so that the liquid that was once well water was once pollen and nectar was once honey and tea and juice was slowly becoming wine.

If the autumn was particularly cold, the yeast in the son's mead would die, and he would need to start over again. If the autumn was particularly mild, the son's mead would be ready for drinking and bottling in a few weeks. But if it was hot and the sun was beating down on the tin shed, and the clouds weren't forming in the skies above and the rain wasn't falling from them, then the son's mead would be ready for drinking and bottling in just a few days.

It was when the mead fermented the quickest that pleased the son the most, because it meant that he could watch the captains and crews at the family's restaurant get drunk and dance under the harvest moon.

~~~

When the bees in their hives clustered around their queens to keep them warm in the dead of winter, the mother would wander around the island, witching wells. With a forked rod in hand, which she had fashioned from the branch of an olive tree, she would walk up and down the dirt footpaths that ran from one end of the island to the other until she felt that rod start to bounce. That rod would start to bounce in her hands so that the tip would jerk down to the ground beneath her feet; this is when the mother knew where to dig her well.

The next day, the family would carry their shovels and pickaxes with them to this spot and dig. They would dig the hole until they came to the water buried beneath the sand and the soil, which would seep through the ground and slowly rise around the feet of the family at the bottom of this freshly dug hole. When this happened, they would construct a wall around that hole with stones that they had carried up from the sea, and at the top, they would build a small well-house with a slanted tin roof, and beneath this roof, they would mount a rope and pulley to haul up water from the depths with a bucket.

Before they found the water, constructed the wall, and built the well-house, they would find things as they dug. Once, they found a giant tree stump, its fossilized roots reaching deep down into the ground below. Another time, they found a pair of massive boar tusks covered in moss. And yet another time, deep down in the ground very close to the aquifer, they found a live sturgeon flopping around in the sand.

But one day, when the family was digging a well, they uncovered something they had never seen before: a flat vinyl disc with the words, THE LAND OF BRIDGES, etched into its surface.

The family stared at this disc for a very long time while standing at the bottom of their hole, but they had no idea what to do with it.

~~~

The daughter had discovered the grooves one night while running her fingers along the disc's surface, and it was the son who had guessed that the disc was designed to spin. So the father pieced together a contraption from scraps and rubbish he either found around the port or traded with the captains and crews that dined in the family's restaurant. He used shells and tin cans; fishing line and needles. And after months of tinkering with it, he called the family into the dining room one night to give it a try.

Inside the dining room, the father cranked the contraption that he had built with his hands, and to his surprise, the disc began to spin. And as it spun, the needle dropped down and dug deep into the grooves—divining a song.

From the shells on the father's contraption came the songs of crickets chirping in the grass. From the shells of the father's contraption came the songs of cicadas, whirling in the pines. From the shells of the father's contraption came the songs of bees, buzzing in their hives.

If the father listened closely, he could hear not only the insects but also the songs of catfish splashing in the back of the cave. And the mother, if she listened closely, could hear the songs of the gushing aquifer running beneath her feet. And the son, if he listened closely, could hear the songs of the mead gurgling in the cellar.

But it was the daughter, imagining the shapes that these bees were taking on as they sang, who could hear the waves crashing on the shores of the island, where crevices in the rocks filled with seawater.

By morning, she knew that the changing tides would have carried all of their shapes back out to sea.

somewhere between the sleet and the snow is the ice. skate across the frozen bay. beneath a whale oil lantern, sip soup on a polar bear rug; through that hole in the floor, fish. when the tide goes out, climb beneath the ice and sing of the city that fell into the sea.

ALONG THE
LUNGOLAGO

What Fills These Shells

Follow the *lungolago*—the road that lines the lake—from Bracciano to Trevignano, and you will see abandoned stables, overgrown vineyards, and waterfront restaurants. In Vicarello, one of these restaurants is made entirely of shells and the people inside built it with their bare hands years ago, when trees covered the hills, before trucks wheeled them away.

These people—a family of four—left Ponza by plane. When they reached the castello that overlooked the lake on the highest hill, they glided down into the crater and skimmed across the surface until they slid into a cove. There they saw the shells scattered in the sand.

The family took one look at these shells and knew just what to do with them. Walking up and down the beach, they picked up the shells and assembled them into a home.

That winter, the clouds hung heavy above the lake until one day, rain leaked through the house of shell and soaked everything inside. But when it did, the family scooped up mud, chopped down reeds along the bank of the lake, and sealed up their home tight.

When spring arrived, the family made a shell mosaic to hang in the window of their home that read: RISTORANTE. They knew the sounds the shells made when the breeze blew through them would say the rest.

~~~

Those with an appetite, biking along the lungolago on their way to Trevignano, Anguillara, or Bracciano, would pull off on the side of the road, dismount their bikes, and walk through the restaurant's doors.

Families would usually sit down at a table in the sand and place their order—a bottle of white wine, a platter of raw oysters, a plate of fried eel, and bowls of spaghetti alla chitarra with perch. Teenagers would nearly always crowd around the billiardino table outside, smoking cigarettes and singing pop songs from the radio. Friends, more often than not, would sit at the bar for a pitcher of homemade beer, out of everyone's way.

But it was always the tourists who would be the first to see them—characters scribbled on yellowed pages, letters scrawled onto leather tomes, symbols etched into blocks of wood.

"What are *those*?" the tourists would ask, stuffing their mouths with eel.

"*Those*," the locals would respond, slurping oysters from their shells and chasing them down with beer, "are *words*."

"*Words*," the tourists would respond, feeling the strange shapes their mouths were taking on. "*Those—are—words*."

~~~

When the moon was full, the mother of the family who built the restaurant from shells would dive down to the bottom of the lake for oysters. Late at night, when the rest of the family was sleeping, she would walk out onto the dock in the back of the cove and stare down into the waters—and then she would jump. Bending her knees and holding her arms high above her head, the mother would dive into the lake and swim down to the oyster beds below.

Most nights, when the mother dove down into the lake for oysters, she would emerge with a sackful of the oval and pear-shaped molluscs. By the light of the kerosene lamp that hung above the sink of the restaurant's kitchen, she would pry the oysters open to see what was inside.

Most nights, what the mother saw were the oysters themselves, sitting in their shells.

But some nights, when the moon wasn't only full but also orange, the mother would see not only the oysters, but their pearls.

It was then that the mother would pluck these pearls from the shells of the oysters and swallow them, one by one, before sitting down in her rocking chair that overlooked the lake and rocking herself to sleep.

~~~

A waning moon meant the daughter was out on the lake, fishing for eels. There was nothing that excited her more than wading in the shallows at night, imagining the long, slim creatures on the lake bottom, feeding—except perhaps for paddling out into the lake to fish for them.

The daughter had learned to fish for eels the same way the mother had learned to dive for oysters—by reading the words that had taken shape on the pages of the books that lined the walls of the restaurant.

From these pages, the daughter had learned where the eels lurked and what they ate. She also learned how to clean and prepare them. But what interested the daughter most, from the pages of these books, was that the town of Anguillara—which she could see across the lake—was the home of Caligula's floating fortress, before it caught fire and sank down in flames to the lake bottom below.

~~~

If the moon was waxing, the son was down on the shores of the lake, collecting rocks. Walking up and down the banks, he would scoop up stones and pebbles and look into them to see what shapes they had taken on.

Some of these stones were smooth and rounded, polished by water passing over them. Some of these pebbles were jagged and rough, cut from a cliff or a cave. Some of these rocks were marbled; others, opaque; others still, obsidian.

All of these rocks, the son had learned from reading the pages of the books that lined the walls of the restaurant, had taken on these shapes both before and after the eruption of the volcano that stood in the lake's place years ago.

The son, after staring into these rocks and seeing what shapes they took on, was assembling them into a mound behind the restaurant, which seemed to grow more and more each day.

~~~

No moon in the sky and the father's up in the mountain springs, searching for salamanders. The words on the pages of the books that lined the restaurant's walls had taught him to never drink from springs unless there was at least one of those glimmering, blunt-snouted amphibians inside.

For years, the father carried buckets and buckets of water from the mountain springs to serve to the diners that stopped in the restaurant while travelling around the lungolago. But one day, a diner sat down at the bar and told the father about an intoxicating elixir made of spring water and fermented grain.

From this day forward, when the father wasn't up in the mountain springs, he was down in the restaurant, flipping through the pages, searching for a recipe for this mystical drink—until one day, he found it—a handwritten list of ingredients, step-by-step instructions, and a crude illustration of a barrel bubbling.

Now that he knew what he needed, he made a deal with the mother, daughter, and son to trade a portion of their oysters, eels, and stones for grain at the local mill. Once he had his grain, he ran straight for the hills, filling up his buckets with as much springwater as he could carry, and then returned to the restaurant, where he started stuffing kindling into the wood-burning stove behind the bar.

~~~

On the night of the lunar eclipse, the daughter paddled the family across the lake to the shores of Anguillara, where they each dropped down their bait: an oyster, an eel, a stone, grain.

It wasn't long before they got bites—the tips of their rods twitching, just as the earth was beginning to cast its shadow upon the surface of the moon above their heads—and once their poles jerked downward, they began to reel.

Each family member stood in the hull of the boat with their feet planted firmly on the floor, their backs arched in the night, their boat rocking in the water as, crank by crank, they heaved whatever they had landed to the surface.

When the moon was nowhere in the sky—just a thin ring of light where it had once hung in the firmament—the lines on the poles in each of their hands went completely slack. Then, to the family's surprise, what surfaced from the depths of the lake was that sunken floating fortress, crawling with eels.

By the time the sunlight reached the surface of the moon again, the family and the fortress were gone.

In the back of the cove behind the restaurant, where the son had piled his stones, a volcano was erupting.

somewhere between the root and the seed is the flower. bike across the rolling fields in spring until your tires pop; there, you'll see bees filling up their pockets with pollen. raise your glass high to them—it is filled with golden mead—and toast to the honeycomb hanging from the trellises, a million buds unfolding into fragrant petals.

What Shapes These Rings

As you follow the *lungolago*—the road that lines the lake—from Anguillara to Trevignano, you will see hilltop castles, ferry boats, and waterfront restaurants. In Bracciano, one of these restaurants is made entirely of sand, and the people inside built it with their bare hands years ago, when pollen blew from pine to pine, before the sap inside their trunks ran dry.

These people—a family of two—left Bracciano by burrowing underground. Driving their shovels into the dirt, they tunnelled beneath the lake until surfacing along the beach on the other side.

The family, upon surfacing, took one look at the beach and knew just what to do with it. Filling their buckets with the wet, firm sand that lined the shore, they carefully assembled these grains—one by one—into their home.

It didn't take long for the snow to fall. But when it did, the family headed up into the hills with their axes and saws to chop down trees for firewood to burn in their hearth. Knowing that passersby would follow the plume of smoke floating out of the chimney into the sky above, the family hung a sign in their window that read: RISTORANTE. They knew the heat that resonated from inside the hearth in the dining room would say the rest.

~~~

Over the years, the restaurant made quite a name for itself—especially among hikers who spent their winters wandering the hills that surrounded the lake. When the wind whipped down the hills and blew across the water, these hikers would walk through the restaurant's doors, eager to sit down by the fireplace with a platter of fried frog legs and smoked trout, as well as a glass of resin wine.

The regulars would walk through the restaurant's doors, take off their snow-covered boots and jackets, and take a seat at the bar; newcomers would stand in the doorway, snow melting into puddles around their feet, until the family invited them to sit down at one of the tables by the fireplace.

But it was always the children who were the first to see them—pine logs, dripping with sap; oak trunks, filled with rings; olive stumps, their knot eyes seeming to gaze into the children's own.

"What are *those*?" the children would ask, their eyes wide and glowing by the light of the fire.

"*Those*," the adults would respond, taking a bite of smoked trout and a sip of resin wine, "are *trees*."

"*Trees*," the children would echo, pulling the meat of the frog legs from the bone, chewing with their mouths open. "*Those—are—trees*."

~~~

Before the family built the day's fire in the hearth, the sister was up in the hills, chopping down trees.

Trees fascinated the sister. She had learned over the years that they could be used for many things: limbs from some trees, when dried out and split into sticks, caught fire quickly and easily in the hearth, making it fine kindling; bark from other trees, when steeped in hot water from the lake, cured headaches; stumps from other trees, when chopped into chips, produced a fragrant smoke, perfect for curing trout caught from the waters of the lake— from the firewood cut from all trees burned in the family's restaurant, fertilizer for the family's garden, which seemed to provide them with more bountiful harvests year after year of ingredients to transform the wine, the fish, and the frogs into something that would keep the hikers coming back for more.

While all parts of all trees fascinated the sister, what interested her the most were the rings that formed inside them—bands upon bands of imperfect circles in alternating shades of brown—and regardless of what kind of tree the sister was chopping down that day, she would kneel down in the undergrowth on her hands and knees to see what shapes these rings had taken on.

Some days, these rings took on the shapes of animals—the eyes of a frog, staring up into the stars that sometimes fell into the lake below. Other days, these rings took on the shapes of maps—streams flowing into lakes flowing into creeks flowing into rivers spilling out into the sea, carrying with them schools of fish. Other days still, these rings took on the shapes of the skies above—clouds rolling across the coast, heavy with rain.

But some days, when the sister stared into these stumps to see what shapes their rings had taken on, she wouldn't only see plants and animals, streams and rivers, clouds and skies—but what came from them as well. And when she did, she would take out her notebook, made from the pulp of the trees that she had chopped down, and write down what she saw in the stump of this tree.

Later that night, she would read this aloud to the embers that burned in the hearth as they slowly became ash. The next day, when she woke up, she would roll a barrel up and down the hills to where she had chopped down this tree. Here, she would drive a nail into the trunk and drain the resin into the barrel, where it would slowly ferment into wine.

~~~

After the fire had gone out in the hearth of the family's restaurant, the brother was out on the lake, fishing for trout and jigging for frogs. There was nothing more that the son loved than smoking this trout and frying these frogs in the kitchen—except for catching them out on the lake at night.

When the family finished cooking and cleaning and the last diner downed their final glass of resin wine, the son would walk out onto the shores of the lake, climb into his wooden rowboat—carved from the trunk of a tree chopped down by the sister years ago—and paddle out into the water.

The brother would begin his night on the lake by trolling for trout. Baiting up two cane poles and letting the line out behind the boat, he would paddle slowly from one bank of the lake to the other. As he rowed, he would imagine what he had heard lay on the bottom below—a sunken floating fortress, a statue of gold, an undetonated bomb—and how the bait attached to the hooks of both poles would be floating above them.

Every so often, while he was lost in thought, he would see the tip of one of his cane poles jerk down. To this, he would drop the oars in the hull of the boat and reel in the fish, lowering it into a bucket of water by his side.

Once his bucket was full, the brother would paddle back to the shallows, where the frogs would be waiting. Standing in the bow, he would stare down into the water until he saw pairs of frog eyes looking back at him. When he did, he would grab his spear and gig these frogs, tossing them into another bucket beside the fish until it too was full.

Later, he would take this trout and these frogs to the kitchen, where he would prepare them for meals. But before he did, he would tie up the boat to the dock at the restaurant and lay down in the hull.

Here, rocking back and forth with the waves, the brother would close his eyes and listen. In the hull of the boat, he would listen to the bats swooping down from the sky above, chasing mosquitoes; he would listen to the fish jumping out of the water, chasing minnows; he would listen to the swans and ducks swimming on the lake's surface, leading their young back into the coves.

While the brother loved all of these sounds that he heard on the lake at night, what interested him most was the sound of the wind blowing through the trees, which always reminded him of the days when he and his sister were raised by their parents by the sea.

~~~

One day, when the sister was up in the hills, chopping down trees, she chopped off one of her fingers. She had raised her axe high above her head and driven it down onto the stump where she was cutting trunks into logs without noticing her hand steadying a piece of wood.

It wasn't until she went to pick up this log and throw it onto the pile that she saw her finger roll off onto the ground. The sister stepped back from the stump and stared at the ground, then stared at her hands. Sure enough, the index finger on her left hand was missing. Leaning over to pick up the finger, she noticed how there wasn't a single drop of blood on the stump or her hand. Staring now at the finger that she held up to the sky, she could not believe what she saw inside.

Inside of her finger were rings—bands upon bands of imperfect circles in alternating shades of brown—and from them, sap slowly seeping down her arm.

The sister stood in the clearing of trees for a long time staring into these rings, mesmerized by the shapes that these rings were taking on.

~~~

The brother looked for the sister every day in the hills that year. He searched the clearings, where stumps sat bare in the weeds. He searched the dense forests, where canopies prevented sunlight from reaching the forest floor. He even searched the shores of the lake, where the fish chased minnows in the shallows and the birds nested in the reeds—but he could not find her.

At night, the brother would still paddle out into the lake and catch trout and gig frogs. When his buckets were full, he would tie up to the dock, lay in the hull, and listen to the bats and the mosquitoes, the fish and the minnows, the fowl and their chicks, and the wind in the trees, until one night, when the harvest moon was full above him, he heard the voice of his sister—faint and cracked—blowing in the breeze.

He followed this voice until he came to a clearing that he had never seen before. In the center of this clearing, there was a stump and the sister's axe lying on the ground. The brother picked up this axe and stared at this stump, then looked around the clearing, only to see trees. He stood there, staring into the surrounding stumps, staring into the surrounding branches, staring into the surrounding leaves, until he noticed that, when he squinted, one of these trees seemed to be reaching for the sky.

The brother steadied his sister's axe in his hands and began chopping down this tree, which he then dragged back to the family's garden behind the restaurant. Here, he set it aflame.

That night, the brother stayed up until sunrise, watching as the embers and smoke rose from the shores to the sky above, the ashes covering every inch of the garden and the surface of the lake, while the morning's breeze blew through the trees.

somewhere between the needle and the thread is the silk. in spring, float down the river until you come to an orchard of trees; there, you'll see them, wrapped in their cocoons. in summer, watch weavers spin strands into thread. in autumn, wrap yourself in sheets—swoon.

These Mushrooms That Glow

W hen you follow the *lungolago*—the road that lines the lake—from Trevignano to Bracciano, you will see sailboats, campgrounds, and water-front restaurants. In Anguillara, one of these restaurants is made entirely of feathers and the people inside built it with their bare hands years ago, when the lake was filled with fish, before they floated belly up.

These people—a family of two—left Trevignano by swimming. Diving from the pier, they swam past the swans and the gulls floating in the shallows until they arrived at a cliff. While wading in the water where waves crashed along the shore, they saw a flight of doves nesting beneath an overhang.

The family took one look at these doves and knew just what to do with them. Collecting reeds from the patches that grew along the banks of the lake, they fashioned them into long handles; gathering grass that grew along the cliff, they wove a net. Laying on their bellies above the overhang with this net held out, the family caught these birds, one by one, until every nest had been emptied.

Some of these doves were kept in cages made of the same woven grass they were captured with. But most of them were prepared for cleaning—their feathers plucked, their meat smoked—and it was with these feathers that the family built their home.

It didn't take long for the wind to pick up on the surface of the lake and scatter the feathers across the hills. But when it did, the family prepared more birds for cleaning and rebuilt their home from the ground up. With more smoked meat than they knew what to do with, they hung a sign in the window that read: RISTORANTE. They knew the view from atop the cliff would say the rest.

~~~

The restaurant never quite made a name for itself. It was on the far side of the lake where few people lived or travelled—except for a ragtag crew of hunters, anglers, and foragers who waded in the waters and wandered about the hills, searching for food.

The family welcomed these people into their establishment, inviting them to bring with them their daily catch in exchange for a roof over their heads, drinks from the bar, and a meal cooked in the restaurant's kitchen. While these people liked the drinks and shelter offered by the family, it was the meal that always had them coming back for more.

The meal served at the restaurant changed daily, based on what was gathered in the hills or caught in the waters. Some days, the hunters carried wild boar and turkey into the restaurant. Other days, anglers carried pike and eel. Other days, the foragers carried in nuts and berries, apples and figs, mussels and clams, wild asparagus and mushrooms. Every day, of course, the father would carry smoked pigeon into the restaurant from the smokehouse out back, just in case the others arrived empty-handed.

But every now and then, a lone straggler wandering the hills, separated from their pack, would walk through the restaurant's doors and join the family and this rowdy crew for a meal. When they did, they would take a seat at the bar, order a drink, and look around. This is when they would see them: the beak of a pelican, filled with sardines; the wings of a chicken, flapping in the wind; the eyes of a crow, seeming to gaze into their own.

"What are *those*?" these stragglers would ask, sipping their beer.

"*Those*," the hunters would respond, gnawing on smoked pigeons, "are *birds*."

"*Birds*," the anglers would echo, spearing a mushroom and twirling pasta around their fork. "*Those* are *birds*."

The foragers, sitting at their table in the corner, sipping honeysuckle mead and ripping meat from turkey legs, would look into the eyes of these stragglers and fold their arms into wings. Then, by the light of the kerosene lamps that hung from the rafters made of bird bone in the ceiling, they would flap these wings and start cawing. These foragers would caw, and cluck, and crow until the hunters and anglers would join them in a song.

It was then that the stragglers, sitting motionless on their stools and staring in awe, would order another round.

~~~

The father of the family who had built the restaurant from feathers was a spear-fisher. When the sun was glowing in the sky, he liked to stand in the shallows of the streams that fed into the lake and spear fish. In the cool water that gurgled up from the ground and flowed over the beds of stones on the stream bottom, he liked to wade, his eyes searching.

Sometimes, the father would spot trout swimming upstream, the cold water flowing into their mouths and out of their gills. Other times, the father would spot bass swimming in the mouth of a creek, waiting for an insect to fall onto the surface from a limb that hung over the water. Other times, the father would spot a crawdad, scurrying from one rock to another.

But regardless of what the father spotted in the stream that day, he would spear them and carry them back to the restaurant, where he would sit at the bar and write.

What the father wrote depended on what he speared in the stream, as well as what the hunters, anglers, and foragers caught and collected in the hills and caught in the waters of the lake that morning.

At the bar, he would write what he had speared—trout, bass, crawfish. And as the gang trickled in, he would write what they were carrying—boar and turkey; eel and pike; nuts and berries; apples and figs; mussels and clams; wild asparagus and mushrooms. And as he wrote, he would begin to see what shapes these words took on.

Some days, the father saw the words take on the shapes of platters—large servings of roasted wild game placed on the tables between the diners to share. Other days, the father saw the words take on the shapes of soups and stews—bowls of hearty meats, fish, and vegetables, swimming in a quick broth rendered from bones, scraps, and trimmings. Other days still, the father saw the words take on the shapes of pasta—handmade spaghetti alla chitarra with sauteed mushrooms in a cream sauce.

When the last of the group would stroll in that afternoon, the father would roll up what he had written on parchment paper, tying it with a blade of grass, then head behind the restaurant, where the doves were kept in their cages.

Grabbing one of the doves and tying the rolled-up parchment paper behind its wings, the father would set the bird free. As he watched it fly across the lake from the cliff to the distant town on the other side, he would wonder whether or not his friend, who would receive the dove in his garden, would paddle across the lake that night to join the family and their guests for dinner.

~~~

The son of the family who built the restaurant from feathers was a forager. When the moon was glowing in the sky, he liked to wander the hills that surrounded the lake or wade in the waters that filled it, foraging.

What the son foraged depended on the season. In the fall, he would pick apples from orchards; in the winter, he would shake nuts from trees. In the spring, he would pull onions up from the ground; in the summer, he would pluck grapes from their vines.

But regardless of the season, the son would always forage fungi.

Mushrooms fascinated the son—their wild, colourful patterns and pungent scents; their spores that fell in powders from their underlying gills, their peculiar tastes and textures. He had learned, over the years, how to identify these mushrooms from the other foragers that came to the restaurant. These odd, quiet people carried with them not only fungi but also books with illustrations and descriptions of mushrooms, along with recipes and stories.

It was from these books—the illustrations, descriptions, and recipes in particular—that the son discovered how to tell one mushroom from another —in their shape, texture, and colour. Some mushrooms, he learned, were good for eating—to be roasted on the grill or sauteed in a pan for sauce. Other mushrooms, he learned, were poisonous—to be avoided under all circumstances. Other mushrooms still, he had read, were medicinal—to be consumed cautiously only in the company of those who knew what they were doing.

But it was from the stories in these books that the son first heard of a mushroom that he had never seen before. These mushrooms, according to the stories, grew in valleys where the wind did not blow. And because there was no wind, the spores of these mushrooms would simply fall from their gills and lay on the ground. But these mushrooms, the writers of these stories said, knew better.

With their mycelia that grew out of their stems, connecting them with other fungi, they communicated. Over time, they learned that mushrooms that glowed in the dark were more successful in spreading their spores. This, they had observed, was due to insects that were attracted by this light, which would search the ground under their caps for prey before carrying the powder across the entire valley—unknowingly aiding in the vast construction of a mushroom kingdom.

When the son first read this, he set out to find them in the dips in the hills that surrounded the lake, carrying with him nothing but a basket made of woven grass. He knew the moon, as well as the mushrooms—if they were there—would light his way.

~~~

The son searched the valleys for the glowing mushrooms for an entire year before he found them. It was after a lightning storm at the height of summer, when he was plucking wild grapes from their vines, that the ground beneath his feet began to glow.

As the sun set into the hills, he wandered around the valley, picking these fungi from the ground and placing them carefully into his basket, which lit up like the kerosene lamps that hung from the rafters made of bone in the restaurant's dining room.

When the son's basket was full, he hurried back, excited to serve these mushrooms to the guests inside.

~~~

The next afternoon, the friend of the father who lived across the lake did not receive a menu from a carrier pigeon. Concerned, he paddled his boat to the cliff and started to climb.

As the friend climbed, he noticed that the restaurant of feathers was glowing a warm, fluorescent green. But it wasn't until he walked through the restaurant's doors that he saw them: perched up on stools at the bar and chairs around the tables were humongous mushrooms, glowing in the dark.

The father's friend stood there for a long time, staring with his eyebrows furrowed and mouth hanging ajar, until he slowly approached one of these fungi to take a closer look while the doves began to coo in their cages outside.

somewhere between the sun and the moon is the tide. sit in the plaza and watch water spill into the streets from the canals. see a pod of dolphins plough through a shoal of mackerel, the leaping fish landing in a fountain of gold.

What Shapes This Sand

If you follow the *lungolago*—the road that lines the lake—from Vicarello to Anguillara, you will see cobblestone streets, wooden docks, and waterfront restaurants. In Trevignano, one of these restaurants is made entirely of bones and the people inside built it with their bare hands years ago, when the skies were filled with birds, before they fell dead in the streets.

These people—a family of two—left Vicarello by foot, walking along the shores until they came to a long, narrow stretch of land that extended far out into the lake. Here, in the mud, they saw animal prints that led into a thick patch of reeds.

The family took one look at these prints and knew just what to do with them. Readying arrows in their crossbows, they followed the tracks until they came to a small clearing, where boars were sleeping in the undergrowth. When the arrows struck these sleeping hogs, they leapt up from the leaves, grunting and squealing. But when they charged the family, the family was ready with more arrows, bringing the wild pigs down to their knees so that they toppled over to the ground.

After letting the blood out of them, the family skinned the carcasses, carved the flesh into slabs of meat, and gathered the bones into a pile. With the skin, the family would make clothes to keep them warm during the winter; with the flesh, the family would make meat by curing it with smoke, sugar, and salt; with the bones, the family would make broth for soups and stew and then lay them out to dry in the sun—with these dry bones, this family built their home.

It didn't take long for the sun to shine brightly on the surface of the lake and make the bones of their home brittle. But when it did, they took their crossbows back into the patch of reeds, returning with more skin, meat, and bones. With their home sturdy and their pantry and closets stocked with more than they knew what to do with, they hung up a sign in the window that read: RISTORANTE. They knew the plume of smoke rising from the chimney, carrying with it the enticing smell of pork, would say the rest.

~~~

Over the years, the restaurant made quite a name for itself. Those with hunger—swimming or floating in the shallows, or sailing or paddling far out in the depths—would smell the scent of pork wafting across the waters, luring them across the lake to the building of bone on the narrow stretch of land.

Swimmers would usually take a seat on the dock, their bathing suits still wet with lake water. Paddlers normally preferred a table inside by an open window. Sailors, more often than not, perched up on stools at the bar, sipping beers and picking at platters of pork.

Everyone saw them—the enormous billowing balls of cotton floating across the sky—but it was the men who rarely knew what they were.

"What are *those*?" the men would think to themselves, their heads bent back and their mouths hanging ajar.

"*Clouds*," a voice would respond in their ears. "*Those—are—clouds. Clouds.*"

"*Clouds*," the men would then repeat aloud, turning to each other, pointing to the skies above. "*Clouds. Those* are *clouds!*"

The women, seated nearby, would simply sip their drinks, imagining bolts of lightning striking from these clouds into the heads of these men, splitting their skulls in two.

~~~

When the wind was blowing, the daughter of the family who had built the restaurant from bone liked to sit at the top of the hill that rose out of the lake and look back at Rome. From her perch, she could see the city—crumbling columns of ancient arenas, elaborate domes of the pilfering church, towering obelisks of the fascist dictator, ominous skyscrapers of the world's banks—and the daughter would carve. Into the bones that the family had taken from the bodies of the boars, the daughter would etch what she saw.

What the daughter etched depended on where and when the wind was blowing. When the breeze was blowing from the west in the spring, carrying the scent of the sea, the daughter would carve images of the Pontine into the bones—willows weeping into saltwater marshes, fish singing in tidal pools. When the breeze was blowing from the east in winter, carrying the scent of the mountains, the daughter would carve images of the Apennine—herds of sheep grazing beneath snow-capped peaks, glacial streams polishing beds of stones. When the breeze was blowing from the north in the fall, carrying the scent of the Piemonte, the daughter would carve grapes hanging heavy on their vines, thermal baths illuminated by the harvest moon.

But when the breeze was blowing from the south in the summer, carrying the scent of the city—coffee and cornetti from caffés, amatriciana and carbonara from trattorias, pollo a la arrosto and salsicce from restaurants—but also the unmistakable stench from the dumpsters on the side of the road, the smog from the cars on the highways, and the odour from whatever carcass was lying at the bottom of the river—the daughter would try her best to carve images of the Eternal City. She really would. But every column, dome, obelisk, or skyscraper—each caffé, trattoria, or restaurant—even the parks, cultural centres, and piazzas—quickly became covered in the trash and the smog and the carcasses, before being swallowed by a pothole becoming a sinkhole in the road.

There was one exception to this, when the daughter could carve images from her stoop atop the mount when the breeze was blowing from the south in the summer: it was when the wind was blowing not only from Rome but all the way from Northern Africa, carrying the sand of the Sahara, which had formed on the floor of a prehistoric sea. It was then that the daughter, with her chisel and bone in hand, could etch the shapes that these clouds of sand took on.

Sometimes, these clouds of sand took on the shapes of caves—mouths gaping at the base of a cliff, caverns leading deep down into the ground below. Other times, these clouds of sand took on the shapes of forests—canopies of trees hanging over a symphony of stones. Other times still, these clouds of sand took on the shapes of the stars—scales weighed down with shells, a porter carrying water, a bull charging into the sea.

But every now and then, these clouds of sand took on shapes of their own. When they did, the daughter would simply stare into them, watching in awe at the shapes that the sand took on.

~~~

If the wind was blowing and it was carrying clouds filled with rain, the mother could be found behind the restaurant with her barrels. These barrels, large and wooden, would fill with the water that fell from the sky, allowing her to make tinctures and perfumes.

The mother discovered how to make these tinctures and perfumes from her daughter, who had taught her about the winds and what they carried—a breeze from the north in the summer could carry mint and juniper, the perfect accent for cocktails; a breeze from the west in the summer could carry salt and jasmine—a pleasant base for a perfume.

But these winds, the daughter had explained, were always changing, and with each change, there was something new to discover—mint and juniper, for instance, may intermingle with oranges if a slight breeze blew in from the south; salt and jasmine may intermingle with pine if the wind blew in from the east. It was for this reason that the mother tended to her barrels before, during, and after every shower or downpour—so that she could study and harness the potential of every drop of rain.

With every season, more and more bottles of tinctures and perfumes lined the shelves of the restaurant. Regulars and newcomers alike were quick to ask what the mother had recently distilled, as well as what she would recommend for pairings. It wasn't uncommon for customers to purchase matching bottles of tinctures and perfumes to use at home. It also wasn't uncommon for customers to recommend the restaurant to friends, family, tourists, or even complete strangers—after all, they wanted to help the family's restaurant succeed.

Unfortunately, this word of mouth is what made it more and more common for the unpleasant men who spoke loudly about the clouds to walk more and more often through the restaurant's doors. These unpleasant men, when they walked through the doors of this family's restaurant, would fix their eyes upon the bodies of the mother and the daughter and gaze. They would gaze and they would gaze—drink after drink, plate after plate—saying offhand remarks to these women. Sometimes, they would say something to the mother about the daughter—or, rather, the body of the daughter. Other times, they would say something to the daughter about the engravings on the walls of the bar, chuckling and pointing at the daughter's visions, which she had etched into bone with her own hands atop the hills that rose out of the lake. Other times still, they would say something to each other, which the mother and daughter would still overhear anyway as they worked behind the bar.

What the women did with these unpleasant men depended on what they said and how they said it. Some would simply be ignored; others would be asked to leave. More often than not, some would be sold a bottle of perfume, convinced it was an enticing cologne—an "aphrodisiac," they would explain—only to discover on Friday night, when spraying it onto their freshly-pressed suit outside the 3-star restaurant where their date awaited inside, that it smelled surprisingly similar to the stench that rose from the dumpsters beneath their apartment windows at the height of summer.

But others—the inexcusable, wretched, disgusting few—were allowed to stay as long as they wanted. After they had gone, paying their bills and driving drunkenly off into the night, the daughter would carve the face of each man into the bones of the boars that the family had hunted on the shores of the lake. The mother, then, would roast these bones in the oven and use them to prepare a hearty broth.

It wouldn't be until they had finished their soup—slurping their bowls dry and sucking every last drop of marrow from each bone while sitting at the bar overlooking the lake—that the mother and daughter both knew that these men would never return.

~~~

Over the years, the trash piled up so high in the city that no one could escape its stench. The daughter, from her perch atop the mount, had watched the heaps grow to such hideous proportions at such an alarming rate that she convinced the mother, who was sick and tired of the reeking perfumes and tinctures that she was able to make from the rainwater that fell from those billowing clouds, that they should do something.

At the height of summer, the daughter took down the bones with her etchings of the clouds of sand from the walls of the bar, while the mother prepared kindling for the stove. Bone by bone, the mother roasted them before dropping them into a stockpot filled with lake water until it came to a roiling boil.

Bringing the stockpot to a slow simmer, the mother and daughter climbed to the top of the mountain that overlooked the city and waited. They waited and waited for the sun to climb high in the sky, until the wind began to blow in gusts from the south.

By sundown, the city was covered completely in sand—except for a solitary stone pine; it stood gallantly on *la collina dell'aventino*, where Remus had once read the language of the starlings as they passed in the sky above.

somewhere between the shell and the bone is the sand. wade out into the surf until the water covers your head; there, you'll see it: a towering castle on the sea floor. look, there's a crab, playing a fiddle; look, there's a flounder, buried in mud. a school of bonito swim overhead. you open your mouth to speak – in swims an eel.

ALONG THE
LUNGOFIUME

What Shapes These Furs

If you follow the *lungofiume*—the road by the river—from Ostia to Garbatella, you will see retention ponds, abandoned apartment buildings, and waterfront restaurants. In Ostia Antica, one of these restaurants is made entirely of styrofoam and the people inside built it years ago with their bare hands, when the town was still a port, before the seas rose above the hills.

These people—a family of three—left Ponza by boat. They sailed across the channel until they came to the mouth of the Tevere, where the river spilled out into the sea. Here, they paddled upstream until they came to a sandbar where styrofoam containers had washed up onto the shore.

The family took one look at this styrofoam and knew just what to do with it. Assembling the pieces into a solid foundation, walls, and ceiling, the family built their home.

It didn't take long for the river to rise. After all, runoff from the paved city streets brought the waters higher than the bridges even during the lightest of rains. So the family tied the building down with rope to trees that lined the shore and hung a sign in the window that read: RISTORANTE. They knew the way the river rocked beneath the feet of the diners would say the rest.

~~~

Over time, the restaurant made quite a name for itself—but only among those curious enough to go by boat. Those floating down the river from the flooded streets of Rome would see the sign in the window, tie up to a cleat on the dock, and walk through the restaurant's doors, their stomachs grumbling.

While those from Roma Nord would usually take a seat by the window, indulging in a decadent feast as they looked out across the marshes, those from Roma Sud would perch up at the bar for drinks and tagliere, staring into the waters below.

Regardless of which part of the city these diners were from, it was always the ones with money who noticed them first: blazing balls of fire floating in the dark abyss.

"What are *those*?" they would ask, sipping prosecco from flutes.

"*Those*," the people without wealth would answer while eating cured meat, "are *suns*."

"*Suns*," the others would echo. "*Those* are *suns*."

~~~

When the moon was low in the sky, the mother of the family who built the restaurant from styrofoam could be found along the banks of the river, hunting nutria. With a net in hand, she would patrol the shores, her eyes carefully surveying the surface of the water, or the mud on the banks, or the reeds in the shallows, until she saw them: those fat, furry rodents with webbed feet and hairless tails.

Creeping down the bank, the mother would approach these mammals, careful not to scare them. Then, crouching in the mud, she would drop her net and pull the plump creatures up onto the banks.

The nutria, grunting and squirming in the net, would try to escape, but the mother would quickly knock them unconscious and throw them into her sack.

By the light of her kerosene lamp, she would clean these nutria in the restaurant's kitchen sink, delicately skinning the carcasses and separating the meat from the bone.

~~~

Before the moon rose in the morning, the daughter, who was a tailor, would be down in her workshop, making fur coats. Over the years, she had worked with many raw materials—cotton, wool, grass, hemp, bamboo—but it was animal fur that she liked to work with the most.

Whenever the mother returned from the river with a sackful of nutria, the daughter would be sitting at the kitchen table, waiting. While the mother cleaned the mammals, the daughter would pay close attention to the markings on the fur, eager to see them under her desk lamp in her workshop.

These markings, the daughter knew, could be read. Like the starlings that flew in murmurations on cold days, or the constellations that moved across the sky on clear nights, there were messages inscribed into the fur of these animals—and the daughter could read them.

Spots around the eye, circles around the tail, stripes along the backbone—all of these could be read by the daughter and then translated into words for the family's ears.

Most of the time, when the daughter stared into these markings, she would see omens for the family—bountiful harvests, rising rivers, thunderstorms. Sometimes, when the daughter stared into these markings, she would see her own dreams—walking barefoot on the riverbottom, clouds of sand blowing across the sea.

But every now and then, when the daughter stared into these markings, they would take on the shapes of their own. When they did, she would take out a pen, and describe the shapes that these furs took on.

~~~

If the moon was high in the sky, the son would be down in his taxidermy studio. While the mother liked to hunt them for food, and the daughter liked to work with their fur, the son preferred to resurrect these fallen rodents to their former state—even if they remained motionless on a shelf.

Standing at his workbench that overlooked the fast-moving currents of the river, the son would reassemble the remaining parts of these animals until a heap of skin, fur, and bone took on the shape of a towering, gallant nutria.

But the son didn't stop there. Out on the banks of the river, he would collect reeds and grass, sticks and branches, lumps of mud and heaps of clay. On the shelves that lined his studio, he would recreate scenes of the nearby riverbank —driftwood lodged between the rocks, sandbanks running along the shore, burrows in the mud where the mammals nurtured their young.

Among these backdrops, the son would mount the bodies of the nutria, their marble-eyes gleaming in the sunlight that entered the room.

One day, when the sunlight was shining through the windows, the moon was high in the sky, and the river was rising from the rains that had fallen in the city that morning, the son swore he saw one of these nutrias twitch.

When he did, he looked up from his workbench and stared this nutria in the eyes. He must've done this for half an hour, until he picked up his bottle of amaro and poured himself another glass.

~~~

On the day of the solar eclipse, the family hosted a massive luncheon. People floated downriver to feast on the mother's decadent nutria stew. People paddled upriver for the daughter's custom-tailored fur coats. People walked across the marshes for the son's taxidermied scenes.

The party began with drinks in the dining room, followed by a fashion show, showcasing the daughter's handiwork. Then came the mother's food— platters of smoked meat, chafing dishes of hearty stews. But as the moon's shadow began covering the sun, the son realized he had left his amaro— which he wanted to toast with when the sky went black—in his studio.

Opening the doors to his workspace, he went to a drawer where his amaro waited, but he noticed something out of the corner of his eye. In the center of the studio, where the scenes were mounted to the shelves, there wasn't a single, solitary nutria perched up on sand, mud, or stump.

In the dining room, the son found them—the guests, the mother, and the daughter—staring out of the large window that overlooked the river. In the pitch blackness of midday, the son watched his nutria—upright on their hindlegs—dancing a waltz on the riverbank.

somewhere between the mist and the dew is the fog. row out into the gulf at daybreak. when the foghorn whistle blows, an octopus tentacle presents you with the shell of a giant clam – in the center: a lustrous pearl.

These Winds That Blow

If you follow the *lungofiume*—the road by the river—from Garbatella to Trastevere, you will see pedestrian bridges, footpaths, and waterfront restaurants. On Isola Tiberina, you will see one of these restaurants made entirely out of cardboard, and the people inside built it with their bare hands years ago, when people still roamed the streets of the city, before they locked themselves inside.

These people—a family of four—left Bracciano by bike. Their tires rolled across the hills and the fields until they arrived at the river, where piles of cardboard lined the shores of an island that divided the waters in two.

The family took one look at this cardboard and knew just what to do. Scaling down the banks of the river and wading through its waters, carrying their cycles high above their heads, they collected the sheets of cardboard and assembled them into a home.

It didn't take long for the townspeople to discover this cardboard shack—which they were not happy to see in their neighbourhood. But the family hung up a sign made of cardboard in the window that read: RISTORANTE. They knew their hospitality would say the rest.

~~~

Over time, the restaurant made quite a name for itself. The townspeople scaled down the banks and waded through the waters, day after day, to eat home-cooked meals prepared by the family's hands. There was fried fish and raw oysters, harvested from the waters that flowed down the river; there was cicoria and spring onions, plucked from the dirt that covered the island; there was smoked quail and roasted dove, caught from the skies that hung above— and there was always table wine and bread, which the family procured from the local alimentari that sat high up on the banks across the river.

While the food and the wine attracted diners day after day to the restaurant, it was the company of the family that interested them most. For when these diners arrived, someone in the family would always sit down at their table and tell tales about the river and what came from it.

Regardless of the tale the family told to the diners that day, there would always be a newcomer who would walk through the restaurant's cardboard doors and take a seat at a table near a window. Here, they would stare around the restaurant until they noticed them—waning gibbouses, waxing crescents, glowing orbs—all hanging from the rafters overhead.

"What are *those*?" the newcomers would ask, stuffing mussels from the river into their mouths.

"*Those*," the locals would respond, sipping white wine, "are *moons*."

"*Moons*," the newcomers would repeat, chewing slowly. "*Those—are— moons*."

~~~

The mother of the family who built the restaurant from cardboard was a river trawler. At night, she could be found out on the river, rowing her boat up and down the banks, trawling the bottom.

When her net was full and she could row no more—feeling the weight of her catch dragging the river bottom below—she would paddle to the shore. In the sand that covered the island's banks, the mother would heave her net to dry land and empty it.

Some nights, what fell from the net into the sand was fish and oysters for the next day's meals.

Other nights, what fell from the net into the sand was trash—heaps and piles of more cardboard, plastic, tin, and glass.

But when the wind was blowing upstream, what fell from the mother's net into the sand would be something she had never seen before—a cylindrical tube, a mechanical bracelet, a magnetic charm.

It was then that the mother would take one look at these things and have no idea what to do with them.

~~~

The daughter was a stargazer. At night, she could be found inside the restaurant, staring into the skies.

Over the years, the daughter had collected the unknown things found by the mother at the bottom of the river and assembled them into an observatory. She discovered that the cylindrical tube, when filled with mirrors and glass, allowed her to see distant objects—like stars, planets, and moons—with ease. She also discovered that the magnetic charm, when marked appropriately, allowed her to determine the directions that these objects were moving. The mechanical bracelet, when wound up, allowed her to keep track of time.

The daughter passed her nights in the observatory with these tools, charting the movements of these objects in the skies above the restaurant on the island.

She would sit up until the early morning hours, sketching her observations on the cardboard walls, sneaking sips of table wine from the barrels in the kitchen.

But every night, before she went to bed, she would step back from her charts and stare at her sketch of one particular object that she had seen through her telescope night after night. This object, even after all the calculations she had made using the cylindrical tube, the magnetic charm, and the mechanical bracelet, was unlike the others. And she couldn't quite determine why.

~~~

The son of the family was a treasure hunter. In the early morning, he could be found on the banks of the river, searching for jewels.

Like the mother, the son knew that the waters of the river had flowed for millennia. But it wasn't the waters that interested the son—it was what the waters carried with them.

The son had heard about the caves that lined the creeks that flowed into the rivers upstream. How they had been carved out of limestone by the currents. How they had been sealed with limestone again. And the son knew that one day the treasure buried in these caves would wash out into the river and return to the island from which it came.

So the son spent his mornings digging, hoping to one day unearth the jewels that had been carefully laid away.

But the only thing the son had uncovered from the sand so far was a book, which his sister discovered in the trash-pile out back in the weeds.

~~~

The father of the family was a discus-thrower. In the afternoons, he could be found at the point of the island, where the waters split in two, spinning his discus.

Some days, the townspeople would come down to the island to throw the discus with the father.

Other days, the family would come out of the restaurant to play with him.

But most days, the father wouldn't play with anyone at all—except for the wind.

After years of living on the island, the father had learned how to play discus with the breeze that blew down the banks of the river and across the water.

He would stay on the point, facing the opposite direction of the wind, and flick the discus with a swift motion of the wrist—and the discus would soar out across the water and then return again into his hands.

The father must've done this every single day since the family moved to the island, until the day that the wind stopped blowing.

~~~

On the day that the wind stopped blowing, the daughter returned to her sketches on the cardboard walls in the observatory in the restaurant. In the centre of all of them was that single, solitary object that she could not crack.

Flipping through the book unearthed by her brother, she quickly skimmed a chapter on the winds. Coming to a section on gravity, her jaw dropped as her eyes returned to the sketches on the wall.

~~~

The family walked out of the restaurant into the hot, humid air that surrounded the island in the river and looked up into the skies.

Above, a massive ball of light was falling to the earth. The family got one glimpse of it before going deaf and blind.

somewhere between the marrow and the flesh is the bone. roast a fish over an open flame. at low tide, place in a stockpot and bring to a roiling boil; reduce heat and simmer. at high tide, serve in the halved shells of coconuts. there you'll see it, taking shape in the fats and oils floating on the broth's surface, shimmering by the light of the moon.

What Shapes This Dough

If you follow the *lungofiume*—the road by the river—from Garbatella to Fiumicino, you will see vacation villas, docked boats, and waterfront restaurants. In Fregene, one of these restaurants is made entirely of sponges and the people inside built it with their bare hands years ago, when the winds whipped down the coast, before they ceased to blow.

These people—a family of four—left Ostia by foot. When they reached the port in the river's mouth, they turned north, where they saw piles of sponges scattered on the beach.

The family took one look at these sponges and knew just what to do with them. With their hands, they assembled them into walls and a ceiling, until they had built their home.

It didn't take long for the rains to soak through them, the water puddling up on the floor beneath the family's feet. But when they did, the family simply squeezed them out and let them dry in the sun.

Knowing their money would soon run out, they hung a sign in the window that read: RISTORANTE. They knew the sand beneath the diners' feet would say the rest.

~~~

Over time, the restaurant made quite a name for itself. Those driving down the lungofiume on their way to the sea would dead-end into the beach and then see the sign in the window before parking their cars and walking through the building's doors.

Couples would usually sit by the window, overlooking the sea. Lone travellers would normally post up at the bar for a drink. Families—especially those with children—would settle for anything they were given, relieved to be out of everyone's way.

But it was the children who saw them first: wisps whipping down the coast; salty breezes blowing through the pines; gusts and gales tossing ships on tumultuous seas.

"What are *those*?" the children would ask, dipping their bread in olive oil.

"*Those*," their parents would explain, wiping tomato sauce from their mouths, "are *winds*."

"*Winds*," the children would respond, slowly chewing on the dough. "*Those* are *winds*."

~~~

The father of the family who built the restaurant from sponge was a gardener. When he wasn't in the restaurant's kitchen cooking or on the restaurant's patio drinking wine, he could be found behind the establishment, walking up and down the rows.

What the father was doing as he walked up and down the garden rows depended on the season. In winter, he would be turning compost into the soil; in the spring, he would be planting seeds. In the summer, he would be tending to plants; in the fall, he would be harvesting crops.

But regardless of the season, when the father walked out of the restaurant's doors with his coffee and strolled down these garden rows, he would always look into the soil and see what he saw.

What the father saw in the soil depended on the day. Some days, he would see sprouts emerging. Other days, he would see mushrooms blooming after a heavy rain. Other days still, he would see animal tracks, leading from a plant to a gap in the garden's gate.

One day, the father saw something he had never seen in the garden's rows before: a small cup made of wood. Not quite sure what to make of it, he carried it inside and washed it out in the kitchen's sink. Fancying its engravings, he then poured himself a glass of wine, which he drank on the restaurant's patio while staring out to sea.

~~~

When the father was walking up and down the garden rows, the daughter was in the barn, milking the goats. Since she was a little girl, she had developed an affinity for these horned, bearded animals. By the time she was a teenager, her mother had made them the daughter's sole responsibility.

What the daughter did with the goats depended on the time of day. In the morning, she would greet the goats with breakfast and milk them. In the afternoon, she would walk them along the marshland, leading them to grass. In the evening, she would clean them—brushing their coarse hair while scratching behind their ears as they bleated.

While she liked all aspects of tending to them, what the daughter loved most was looking into their eyes. The eyes of these goats were unlike any other eye the daughter had ever seen before. Most animals that the daughter had seen had round eyes with round pupils; however, these goats were different. Their eyes, she had first discovered when she was a little girl, were round with rectangular pupils—and this puzzled the daughter immensely.

As she yanked and pulled on their udders in the morning, she would stare into them, imagining the shapes that their world took on.

~~~

If the daughter was in the barn, the son was in the chicken coop.

The son loved chickens. He loved greeting them in the morning and closing the coop up at night; he loved watching them roost in the fig trees in the afternoon and scratch in the dirt in the evening.

There were few things that the son loved more than the chickens themselves

—except for cooking and eating them. The restaurant had developed a reputation over the years for the son's chicken. Diners would come from all around to feast on the feathered birds—from buckets of fried legs and baskets of wings to blackened breasts and jerk thighs—and they all agreed: the boy's chicken couldn't be beat.

But before the son cooked the chicken for the lunch crowd, he would begin his day in the coop. Most days, he would collect the eggs for the mother, who would bake them into her bread. Most days, as well, he would pick a chicken for himself to clean and prepare in the restaurant's kitchen for lunch.

But some days, before the son would collect the eggs or pick a chicken, he would have taken care of something else. Walking out of the restaurant's doors with his coffee in hand, he would hear it before even opening the coop: the entire brood, clucking wildly inside the thin wooden walls. When opening the door, he would see them perched up in a high corner, flapping their wings and walking in circles. Where the chickens slept would be a snake, filled with eggs as it slithered in the straw.

The son would take one look at this snake and know just what to do with it. He would simply pick it up by its tail and walk it right back into the restaurant's kitchen.

Those days, for lunch, there was a sign in the restaurant's window that read, in bold black letters: SNAKE & EGGS. It was second only to the chicken for regulars and newcomers alike.

~~~

The mother was a baker. All day long, every day of the year, she could be found in the kitchen, baking bread. What the mother baked into the bread relied on what the father, daughter, and son brought in from the garden, barn, or coop that day. Some days, she would bake rosemary into her baguettes. Other days, she would glaze her loaves with eggs. Other days still, she would fold butter into her batter for biscuits.

Regardless of what the mother baked into her bread, she would always add some of her homemade yeast to the dough so that it would rise. Sitting on the windowsill above the wood-burning stove, the dough would rise in a bowl greased with butter. After it had risen, the mother would drop that doughball out on the counter, punch it down, and get to kneading.

It was when the mother kneaded that she would wait to see what shapes the dough took on.

Some days, the dough took on the shapes of driftwood that had washed up on the beach in front of the restaurant. Other days, the dough took on the shapes of vinyl records, like her mother's mother had listened to when she was a little girl. Other days still, the dough took on the shapes of mushrooms, bulbous caps billowing over the countertop before being baked in the oven underneath.

But every now and then, this bread would take on the shapes of its own. And when it did, she would sketch them out in her notebook, which she kept in a cabinet with the flour and yeast. That night, she would gather wet sand on the beach and build sandcastles in the shapes of this dough. By the morning, she knew they would be gone.

~~~

The father saw it first. He had just finished the wine in his wooden cup when the seas retreated from the shore. The mother saw it next—the dough rising ever so high in the kitchen. The daughter saw it, too, inside the barn—curling in the eyes of the goats.

But the son, who was frying chicken on the restaurant's back porch for lunch that day, as the wings were sizzling in the oil and he was staring longingly into a freshly-fried wing, dripping with hot sauce, neither saw nor heard anything at all.

The towering wave simply crashed onto the land, carrying the restaurant of sponge, the family, animals, and crops out to sea.

somewhere between the salt and the smoke is the fish. sail across the sea until you arrive at the island with a rocky coast; there, you'll see it, hanging from a cliff: a wall of fillets suspended from a ceiling of bone.

What Shapes These Notes

F ollow the *lungofiume*—the road by the river—out of Rome and you will see abandoned forts, towering churches, and waterfront restaurants. Along the canals of Pigneto, one of these restaurants is made entirely of plastic and the people inside built it with their bare hands years ago, when the sky was filled with clouds, before the companies sent them away.

These people—a family of four—left Isola Tiberina on foot. Walking along the river until they came to the flooded railroad tracks—where there was a canal—they arrived in the village where plastic was piled up on the banks.

The family took one look at this plastic and knew just what to do with it. Assembling plastic pipes into a frame and draping sheets of plastic on top, they built their home.

It didn't take long for the sun to shine on this house of plastic, inviting seeds to sprout in the warm soil. When it did, the family gathered more plastic pipes from the banks to irrigate these plants and then hung a sign in the window that read: RISTORANTE. They knew the crops harvested inside would say the rest.

~~~

Over time, the restaurant made quite a name for itself. The villagers who wandered up and down the canal with bottles of wine and baskets of bread were drawn into the restaurant's doors by the scents of the plants that grew inside—tomatoes hung heavy on their vines; spinach, arugula, green onions, and garlic carpeted the floor; cucumbers and zucchini hung from trellises;

olive, orange, and fig trees reached for the sky; watermelons fattened in the weeds.

These villagers would take a seat wherever the family would sit them, and then they would begin uncorking their wine, slicing their bread, and placing their orders for their feast.

But it wasn't only the villagers who wandered into the restaurant. Every now and then, a tourist would get lost in the Eternal City and end up in the village of Pigneto. Following the scents of the plants into the dining room, they would stand in the doorway, staring in confusion at what was inside—clouds of mist falling from the ceiling; drops of dew sliding down stems; puddles of rain pooling up in the soil.

"What is *that*?" the tourists would ask, squinting their eyes in the mist.

"*That*," one of the villagers would respond, taking a big swig from a bottle of wine and spreading tomato onto a sliced baguette, "is *water*."

"*Water*," the tourists would echo, opening their mouths to allow the mist to settle on their tongues. "*This—is—water*."

~~~

The father of the family who built the restaurant from plastic was an upright bassist. In the evening, he would be in the dining room, playing his bass. With his toes in the mud, the green onions and garlic growing around his feet, he would thump the sheep-gut strings with the fingers of his right hand, the fingers of his left hand moving up and down the fingerboard so that the low notes would resonate inside of the body of the instrument and spill out of the f-holes into the dining room around him.

The way the father would move his fingers on the strings depended on what was happening inside of the restaurant that night. On nights when seeds sprouted, the father would move his fingers on the strings so that arpeggios rose out of the body of the bass, causing stems to shoot out of the soil. On nights when limbs hung heavy, the father would move his fingers on the strings so that crescendos rose out of the body of the bass, causing the fruit to fall to the ground.

But it was on nights when the flowers opened that the father would move his fingers on the strings so that a waltz rose out of the body of the bass, inviting honeybees to drink the nectar while the villagers danced on their toes by the light of the moon.

~~~

The mother of the family who built the restaurant from plastic was a harpist. Late at night, she would sit on the banks and pluck her harp.

The notes the mother played on the harp depended on the shape of the moon in the sky that night.

If the moon was a waxing gibbous, she would play ascending scales, her fingers moving swiftly from the low strings to the high.

If the moon was a waning crescent, she would play descending scales, her fingers moving slowly from the high strings to the low.

If the moon was full, she would play diminished chords, rarely resulting in resolves.

But if the moon was nowhere in the sky, the mother wouldn't play anything at all. She would simply lay down on the banks of the canal and stare into the stars until she fell asleep.

~~~

The son of the family who built the restaurant from plastic was a trumpet player. In the afternoon, he would walk up and down the banks, blowing his horn.

The villagers, hearing the notes floating up from the canal, would wander down to the banks to watch him play. And while they enjoyed listening to the music that came from the trumpet, what brought these people down to the canal day after day was what these notes did to the water.

Some days, the notes from the trumpet would invite baitfish—and with them, larger fish—to the surface, the canal coming to a roiling boil.

Other days, the notes from the trumpet would invite birds—gulls, herons, and doves—to the banks, their calls unifying in song.

Other days still, the notes from the trumpet would invite the villagers into the waters, where they would bathe naked in the afternoon sun.

~~~

The daughter of the family who built the restaurant from plastic was a singer. In the early morning, she could be found high up on the canal banks, singing songs.

These songs—according to the few and far between who had seen them being sung—did things to the waters of the canal.

The baker, preparing baguettes in the bakery before sunrise, saw the daughter singing one morning, the waters of the canal curling into high ocean waves on the banks.

The winemaker, sipping a final glass of red before heading to sleep, saw the daughter singing another morning, the waters of the canal splitting in two— fish flopping wildly on the dry canal bottom below.

~~~

Every winter, when the plants in the restaurant of plastic lay dormant, the family would sit out on the banks of the canal and play music together. The villagers, hearing the music floating up from the canal, would climb down the stairs of their apartments and wander down to the banks below, carrying bags of bread and bottles of wine. They would all sit out in the cool winter air and lift their voices in song, which caused the waters of the canal to rise into the sky and form clouds, carrying their voices out to sea.

somewhere between the beak and the bird is the feather. fly over the mountains until you see a nest perched atop a tree; there, you'll see it blowing in the breeze. pluck a plume from the wall and dip it in the well of ink—scribe.

These Words That Bloom

F ollow the *lungolago*—the road that lines the lake—until you arrive at a restaurant made of books.

Walk through this restaurant's doors, and you will see the poet that built it, reading words out loud from pages pasted to the walls.

The poet had left Rome on the day the sky had filled with words, following their murmurations out of the city until they dove down to the lake bottom below.

~~~

From that day on, the poet dove down into the lake after the words to see what they could find.

Some days, the poet would emerge from the lake with a basket full of freshwater oysters. Other days, the poet would emerge with bottles of prosecco. Other days still, the poet would emerge with nothing.

But when the sky was filled with clouds and the sun was hidden behind them, the poet would emerge with clusters of letters tangled in fishing line, netting, and kelp.

Back at the restaurant's bar in the afternoon light, the poet would detangle these clusters of letters, arranging them this way and that until they had assembled a word.

The poet would do this, stringing together these letters into words as the sun sank down behind the hills, until they had composed a poem.

~~~

The shapes these poems took on depended on the shapes of the letters that the poet had emerged with that day.

Some days, the poems took on the shapes of the clouds that floated above the lake, heavy with rainwater from the sea. Other days, the poems took on the shapes of the stars that glided across the sky, rising and falling into the hills. Other days still, the poems took on the shapes of the trees that grew along the banks, their roots reaching down into the soil.

Regardless of what shapes the poems took on, the poet would always read them aloud in the restaurant that night while serving oysters on the half-shell and pouring flutes of prosecco for the diners.

~~~

The diners liked the oysters and the prosecco served by the poet in the restaurant made of books, but what brought them back to the lake, night after night, were the words.

The words of the poems, as the poet read them aloud, would fill the ears of the diners and slide down the back of their throats, where they would plop down into their bellies.

Depending on the shapes of these poems—as well as what else was inside of the diners that day—one of three things would happen to the words in their bellies.

For most, the words would simply slosh around with the oysters and the prosecco as the poet sat on a stool and read on.

For some, the words would sprout in their bellies like seeds before digesting with the food and the drink as they sat at their tables and talked into the late hours.

But for the few and far between, the words would not only sprout in their bellies—but grow.

When the words would sprout and grow, the few and far between would feel something creeping up the back of their throat as the poet read the words out loud in the restaurant that night.

Then, all of a sudden, as the poet read the last line and raised their flute in a toast, the jaw of this diner would drop open, a freshly-bloomed bouquet of jasmine flowers hanging between their lips.

The diners, staring in awe at the few and far between, the restaurant now filling with the sweet smell of spring, would watch as the poet would pluck the petals from the bouquet and drop them delicately into the flutes of the diners, finally raising their glasses to the sky.

somewhere between the flour and the heat is the bread. in the morning, grind grain. in the afternoon, mix warm water with yeast – let it rise. in the evening, knead into a loaf and bake. there, you'll smell it, wafting out of the kitchen window as you sit on the terrace, watching the wind blow in a storm.

What Shapes This Wood

They came from the sea.

some crawled,

others swam.

others still stood on their hind legs,
staggering into the dunes.

out of the surf they leaped
into tidal pools.

into the mud they flopped
out of the canals.

some say, from the planks of sunken ships.

others, from the limbs of fallen trees.

others still, from spewing vents or cooling seeps,
deep down in the trench.

sometimes, we hear them singing in the caves.

other times, we watch them staring into the clouds.

other times still, we dance with them in the sand,
the rising tide carrying us back out to sea.

www.ingramcontent.com/pod-product-compliance
Lightning Source LLC
Chambersburg PA
CBHW050349030726
47503CB00008B/2698

* 9 7 8 1 0 6 8 8 6 3 7 1 4 *